WELCOME TO COOLERSVILLE

CAREY HARDISKY

WITCHES OF COOLERSVILLE

BOOK ONE

ABOUT THE AUTHOR

Carey Hardisky is the author of the serialized fantasy adventure, *Adventures of Thira*, a short story, *One More Day, Misadventures of a Mom Author*, the non-fiction project where she chronicles her writing journey while parenting and other responsibilities, and the urban fantasy series, *Witches of Coolersville.*

Her love of storytelling started with making up stories with her sister playing dolls; now, she's writing down her stories to share with the world.

When she's not writing or participating in the writing community on YouTube and Twitch, Carey can be found with her family and friends, prepping for the next Renaissance festival, or crocheting something new.

Carey lives in a quiet neighborhood near Cleveland, Ohio. Follow Carey Hardisky on her writing journey or connect with her on social media: https://linktr.ee/CareyHAuthor

ACKNOWLEDGMENTS

A special thank you to everyone who made my publishing dream possible. My support network: My parents, sister, husband, little girl, aunts and uncles, Veronica - my sister from another mister, all my friends on Authortube: Charlie, Kat, Glory, Tom, Laura, Megan, Jayce, Haley, Eva, Chandra, Mama Magie, Sako. And so many more.

Special thank you to Charlie who helped design the cover and guided me through the process and Ray for helping with formatting.

For Veronica - my bestie. All those roleplay sessions helped make this story possible.

CONTENTS

CHAPTER 1

TARA SAT IN HER ROOM, SURROUNDED BY THE SCENT of musty cardboard and plastic totes. Her life was reduced to a pile of stuff. A laundry pile the size of Mount Everest sat next to her bed. As sweat ran down her neck, she muttered under her breath about why her parents still didn't have central air conditioning. She grabbed a rubber band off her wrist, pulling her long, red hair into a loose bun. She stood, stretched, and went downstairs.

The sizzle of something frying made her stomach growl as the sound reached her ears. The intoxicating smell of chicken, garlic, and rosemary wafted from the kitchen. She turned the corner and saw her mom throwing slices of potatoes into a pot to deep fry.

"Taking a break?" Mom asked, not looking up from the pile of potatoes on the cutting board.

"Yep," said Tara. She grabbed a water bottle from the fridge and held it to her neck. She leaned against the counter and sighed as the cool plastic offered some much-needed relief.

Tara was about two inches taller, so her mom looked up ever so slightly as they talked. They shared eye color, a bright green, some facial features, like round face and long neck, along with a similar curvy figure. "I'm almost done," Tara said. "I just needed to cool off a bit. I'd like to load the car up tonight so I can just go in the morning."

Mom returned her focus to her cooking but sighed heavily.

Tara rolled her eyes. The plastic crinkled in her hands as she forced herself to not react and take the bait her mother was laying out, inviting a fight. "What?"

"You're in that much of a hurry to leave?" Mom asked. "I don't understand why you won't wait until it's closer to the semester starting. You can just move down there at the end of the summer like everyone else. Do you even know what your major will be? You can always go to where Dad teaches for a while, get your basic courses, figure things out, and then go somewhere even better."

Tara clenched her fist around the water bottle, forcing it against the nape of her neck again, easing into the relief the cold bottle provided. She took a deep breath and tried to think of how, once again, to have this seemingly repetitive conversation with her mother.

Tara had been accepted to Continental College. It was a school located in the very small town of Coolersville, about 2 hours south of where they lived in Cleveland, Ohio. Tara dreamed of going there since she was a little girl. Dad had been a student there, just like her grandparents. It was something of a Kavanagh family tradition, she thought. Her father and sister were thrilled when she had received her acceptance letter, along with a full scholarship. And then there was her mom.

Mom seemed to be on a mission to keep her daughters away from her in-laws. She never gave a clear reason why. It didn't make sense. Gran was one of the sweetest people Tara knew. She was hard-working, generous, and always told great stories. Yet, for some reason, she clashed with her daughter-in-law.

Tara finally spoke up. "I thought I could spend some more time with Gran. And she offered me a job."

Tara's mom dropped the knife against the cutting board as she looked up, shocked and angry. "What kind of job? When were you going to tell me? Why on earth would she do a thing like that?" she sighed heavily.

Tara stepped back and held up her hands. "Calm down. She just called me an hour ago. I was going to tell everyone when we had dinner. It's at the gift shop she owns. She said she's short-staffed, and the summer is the tourist season.

"Isn't there someone else she could hire instead?" Mom asked.

"It's a small town," said Tara. "Everyone probably already has their own thing."

Before the argument could continue, they heard the front door open and a dog's frenzied barking. Dad and Christine, Tara's 13-year-old sister, were finally home. Tara leaned against the counter. Relief washed over her. The tension in the air was so thick you could cut it with a knife. Maybe they would be a distraction from this conversation.

Christine, covered in brown dust from her softball game, raced through the house laughing as Mickey, their German short-haired, ran at her heels. There was a dog park near the ballfield so Dad would take Mickey to run around while Christine had games or practice. "Hi, Momma. Hi, Nerd," Christine called as she bolted out the back door.

Dad stood behind his wife, wrapping his arm around her waist and nuzzling her neck. She squirmed as his beard tickled. "If I cut my fingers, it's your fault," she teased, waving the knife.

He stepped back and stuck out his lip in an exaggerated mock pout. "Okay, fine." He started to walk away when she whirled around and kissed him on the cheek. He beamed and pinched her butt. He smirked when he saw Tara watching them. His dark brown eyes twinkled with a bit of mischief. "What?"

"Nothing," said Tara, smiling. "Just admiring how cute you two are." She put the water bottle back in the fridge. "How much longer until dinner? I want to finish more upstairs."

"Less than 10 minutes," said Mom.

Christine raced back through the kitchen. "I need to shower!"

"Put your dirty clothes in the wash, too!" Mom called.

"How was the game?" Tara asked her dad as they fell into their dinner prep routine.

"Okay," he said. He handed Tara a stack of plates. "The usual drama ensued with the coach's daughter. Another girl wanted to pitch, and she lost her mind."

"Let me guess," said Tara, rolling her eyes. "He gave in?"

"After she spent half the game in the car screaming like a toddler," Dad said. "I tried to argue in the other girl's favor. She was doing really well. Then, Jen gets in and cuts their lead by half in her first inning. They won, but barely."

Tara and Dad laid out plates, utensils, and condiments as Mom pulled things out of the oven. The kitchen was small, but not to the point that 3 people were overcrowded. Tara was nearly as tall as her father at 6 feet but ducked and weaved through to the dining room without colliding with anyone or anything.

A typical Sunday evening at the Kavanagh household. Dad moved the papers he had been grading off to the side. He was a history professor at a community college and liked to spread out across the table to work when not in his cramped office on campus. Christine returned and grabbed everyone's drinks. Her baseball uniform changed to shorts and a tank top. Her short brown hair was still damp and dripping down her neck, but she didn't seem to care.

Tara's stomach roared as everyone settled in for the meal. Smells mixed and filled the room. Baked chicken with garlic and rosemary, the crispy skin glistened in the light of the room. Steam rose from a giant pan of macaroni and cheese, still bubbling around the edge. The potatoes were cut into thin slices like chips, fried to perfection, then coated in salt and ranch dressing mix for delicious flavor.

"So," Dad said as he poured the hot sauce on his chicken. "Are you all ready to go?"

"Just about," Tara said. "I just need to pack up the rest of my clothes and bring everything downstairs."

"And don't forget to tell everyone about your grand announcement," Mom grumbled.

Dad and Christine looked at Tara expectantly. Tara managed not to roll her eyes at the clear passive-aggressive comment filled with the all too familiar irritation in her mom's voice. "Gran called me while I was packing and asked if I wanted to work at the gift shop."

"That's great news," said Dad. "She's really needed help since Lorraine got sick."

"Is Lorraine that nice lady with the candy behind the counter?" Christine asked as she heaped the mac and cheese onto her plate.

"And in her purse and probably every room in her house," said Dad, chuckling. "She loves her sweets. The nursing home she's at has a strict no sugar policy, so Gran is always sneaking her some sweet goodies."

Christine giggled. Tara made a face and said, "I don't think I could live somewhere that didn't allow sugar."

Mom spoke up. "It's ridiculous that she has to leave so many months before school."

"It's not even 3 months," Tara said. "The semester starts at the end of August."

"And there isn't a job on campus you could get?" Mom asked. She glared and gestured with her fork. "Like the book store or the cafeteria? Or the tutoring center? Did you even bother to look?" She paused, thought for a moment, and then continued. "Or, how about this? Forget working. Focus on your studies and we'll just load money onto your debit card.

College is going to be a big reality check for you... it's not easy."

Tara struggled with how to respond. This was the same lady who thought $5 per day was enough for lunch when Tara was in high school. While everyone enjoyed a full plate lunch, Tara had a bag of chips and a bottle of soda pop. Then Mom wondered why Tara went right for the fridge when she stepped off the bus.

Knowing where this was going, as the debate had been going on since Easter, Dad raised his hands slightly to quiet everyone. He turned to his wife and gently laid a hand on her knee. "Michelle, honey, I know you're worried." He tried to keep his voice calm and even. "This is Tara's first time away for a long time. I'm nervous, too. But she wants to take this step and it'll be good for her to start being on her own. She's only a couple of hours away and we can be there if she needs anything. It's not like she's going halfway around the world or something. There are things to do, and organizations she can join to get the full college experience. You remember how much fun we had there, right?"

"Wait, what?" Tara exclaimed. "Did you go there, too?"

"No!" Mom said a bit too quickly.

Dad sighed and turned to Tara. He stayed in the same even tone. He continued as if his wife had never reacted. "Look, to put your mother's mind at ease, I'm going to lay down some ground rules.

"Okay," said Tara.

"I want a check in text once a week," he said. "Group chat with me and your mom, so we both get it."

"No, make it daily," Mom said. "And a call once a week." She said, emphasizing with the fork in her hand.

Dad opened his mouth to debate, but Tara spoke up. "That's fine." *Anything,* she thought, *to try to keep peace with her.* She continued out loud, "It's not hard to set a reminder on my phone in the mornings."

"Alright then," said Dad. "A text daily, and a call once a week. Let us know if you have problems or if Gran needs anything. She says she doesn't want to worry us, so you need to be my eyes and ears. When school starts, keep up with your studies. I think Gran mentioned that she has another young lady who is also a student, so she's good at working around schedules and will limit hours if you need extra study time."

Tara nodded. "Got it." Believing the matter to be finally settled, Tara put her plate in the sink and went upstairs to bring down what was already packed while everyone cleaned up. When she started taking things outside, Mom followed and tossed boxes haphazardly into Tara's small SUV. Worried something was going to break, Tara rearranged some of the banged up boxes.

Mom stopped suddenly. "What?" she snapped, a furious look on her face. "Not good enough for you?"

Tara stopped for a moment to stare at her mother. "What are you talking about? I'm just making sure everything fits and nothing gets broken."

"If you would listen to me, we wouldn't need to do this at all," her mother shouted.

Tara's cheeks flushed hot as she caught a couple walking their dog past the house. They hurried their pace at the sound of raised voices.

"Mom, please," Tara begged. She set her box down and took a step closer. "Calm down. I appreciate your help. I have some things I don't want to get damaged."

"Do it yourself, then," Mom snapped. She dropped the box she was holding onto the driveway and stormed off into the house. The door slammed behind her.

Tara just managed to stifle a scream as the glass shattered at her feet. The box her mother was holding was marked "Candle Jars." Tara had painted some jars and put little battery tea lights inside to decorate her room. There were also picture frames in the box that were likely cracked.

Christine came outside. "Are you okay? What happened?" she gently asked, placing a hand on Tara's shoulder.

Tara couldn't speak. She shook her head and continued to load the car as she fought, and failed, to hold back her tears. The salt stung at her eyes as they streamed onto her face. When she was done, she thanked her sister for helping her finish, wiping the tears from her cheeks onto her dirty t-shirt, and raced up to her room to sob.

Tara carelessly tossed clothes into suitcases just to get things off her bed. There was a knock on the door. Tara remained silent, thinking it was her mother with another lecture.

"Hey, sis. Can I come in?" a soft voice asked.

Tara turned to see Christine peeking around the door. She nodded and moved her clothes to make room on the bed. Christine carefully made her way across the cluttered floor and Tara's gaze caught the large box in her sister's arms. "What's that?" she asked.

"I made something," Christine said, beaming. She held out the box as she sat down. "It was supposed to be ready for graduation, but I didn't get all the pages done."

Tara took the box and opened it. Inside was a scrapbook almost full to bursting with pages. Underneath was a thick envelope of more pictures, packs of stickers, and more paper. Each page in the scrapbook was beautifully decorated to highlight the memories in the photos. Her sister had such an eye for detail. Tara felt the familiar catch in her throat as tears threatened to flow once more. "Thank you," she managed, as she pulled Christine into a hug.

"The book is mostly to keep the pages nice. I thought you could hang them in your dorm room or your room at Gran's," Christine suggested. "And the extra stuff is there so you can add on."

"That's fantastic!" Tara exclaimed.

"Do you want some help with this?" Christine asked. She scrunched up her nose and gestured around the room. "It looks like your closet threw up."

Tara laughed. "Sure."

They started folding clothes and arranging things in the suitcases so it all would actually fit. As they worked, Tara let out a sigh. "God, everything is such a mess."

"Just please talk to Mom in the morning so you don't leave on bad terms," said Christine. She held up a black laced blouse. "Do you still want this? It's cute."

Tara snatched it away. "Yes. That's why it wasn't in the bag I gave you Friday. You had your chance to raid my closet." She tucked it away quickly before she continued. "Do you think she's right? Am I making a mistake?"

Christine shrugged. "I don't know. I think all the stuff she says about Gran is wrong, and I don't know how Dad puts up with it."

"Yeah," said Tara. "Did you notice when Dad mentioned being in school? She was real quick to deny his story. But it wasn't the time to push it."

"Yeah, I did. That was weird. But you have a great chance at this school." Christine went on. "You got a full scholarship. And a summer with Gran! I'm honestly jealous. Just make sure you clear things with Mom or it'll be, at best, really awkward next time you see each other. At worst, things will just keep getting worse. Plus, I really don't want to hear her complaining all summer about it through her heaving sighs." Christine rolled her eyes.

Tara laughed, nodding, and they continued working away with minimal conversation. When the suitcases were stuffed until it was difficult to close them, they hauled them to Tara's car. Dad helped with some of the heavier ones. Mom was already in bed. When the car was fully loaded, Tara hugged her sister and dad, said good night, and went back to her room.

She went to the bathroom and popped a pain pill to fight off the headache that usually threatened after she had been crying a lot. Her eyelids felt like they had weights tied to them with how heavy they were. She winced at her reflection when she saw the blotches on her face from crying and the dark circles under her eyes. Tomorrow had to be better. As Tara's head hit the pillow, she slowly drifted off and began to dream.

She stood in the middle of the woods. The moon shined like a lantern through the trees, gently glowing to guide her path. Leaves and sticks crunched underfoot as she walked. She heard night creatures rustling in the bushes as she passed by. The distant howl of a wolf, an owl screeching, bats squeaking. The trees were full and highlighted a deeper green than she had ever seen in her life.

The path led on further into the woods. It felt like she had traveled miles and yet that no time had passed at all. The path twisted, turned, and went up and down small hills.

As she moved, sights and smells shifted into each other and gradually changed. The trees thinned out to reveal the entrance of a clearing. The distinct smell of a bonfire in the air that brought her back to grade school camping trips. Herbs or an incense of some kind burned along with the wood. Tara could pick out scents like sage, rosemary, and a sweet lingering vanilla in the mixture.

She entered the clearing and stopped short, gaping at the sight before her. The ground was lush with tall grass and flowers. A mountainous bonfire blazed in the center. The pile of wood stacked to burn was as tall as she was. Flames licked toward the tree tops, casting the entire clearing in a strange, but comforting, familiar glow. The flames were not the orange and yellow of the many backyard party fires Tara was familiar with. It was bright ocean blue and bluish green in the center. The heat was so strong it warmed her skin where she stood several yards away.

A group of hooded figures stood in a circle around the blaze holding hands, singing in a strange language. Their shadows dancing against the flames of the fire casting an eerie ghostly presence behind them. Tara didn't understand the words, but the perfect melodious harmony of female voices was haunting and beautiful. In the back of her mind, kind of familiar. Like a sound from a dream or long ago memory. It sounded like some kind of beautiful prayer. The haunting melody was upbeat and she could hear the joy in their voices.

Outside the circle, others watched and sang along. Some children were even dancing. Tara stepped closer and could see a few faces clearer in the moon and firelight. The women in this group ranged in age from small toddlers clinging to the skirts of their mothers to women who looked older than Gran. They wore simple white dresses, some had ropes tied around their waist for a belt. Some of the children wore flower crowns on their heads.

Tara wondered what kind of ceremony or ritual this must be. And why did it touch her so? It wasn't sad. She could see that clearly enough. Even though she didn't know what they were saying, she knew the words were loving and happy. This was a true celebration of life.

Tara was so mesmerized by the scene before her that she was oblivious to the harsher sound coming through the trees. A gunshot pierced the serenity of the night and shook her to her bones. Her heart skipped a beat and then sped up as the surrounding women stopped singing and looked around. Some cried. Tara stood paralyzed as men with weapons and torches swarmed in from every direction.

The women shrieked and screamed as they were apprehended. Some tried to run. Others grabbed fallen branches to fight back, protecting those who were too old or young to fend for themselves. Sobs mixed with screams as a pair of girls were pulled out of each other's arms by some of the men.

Someone dropped a torch and the flames caught the grass and trees. Mixing with the fire of the torches, the flames turned to dark blue and purple as they began their ravenous destruction. Sheer panic erupted. Women screamed. Men shouted. The moon was lost behind a heavy drape of black smoke. And, somewhere in the distance, a voice shouted...

"Tara, wake up!"

**Wake up? What?* She felt a hand grab her. Fearing it was one of the men with weapons, she reacted. She cried out and thrashed with all her might.*

CHAPTER 2

Tara felt a hand grab her wrist. She sat up and screamed, flailing wildly. Was she being captured, too? How did they see her?

It took a minute for Tara to realize she was in her room. Her mom's arms came around her and she snuggled into the embrace for a minute to calm down. She closed her eyes as her mom stroked her hair like when she was little. She was safe. She was home.

"It's okay," Mom soothed. "You were just dreaming. It's alright. Take a breath. In and out. That's a girl."

"What's all the noise?" Christine stood at the doorway yawning. Her brown hair stuck up in all directions, rumpled pajamas, eyes barely open but enough to glare at her sister.

Tara felt the heat rise in her cheeks. "I just had a dream."

Christine sighed and muttered something about needing coffee as she shuffled out and down the hall. Tara smiled. Her sister was not a morning person. Every day during the school year was a battle to get her going, so she didn't miss the bus.

Tara pulled away from her mother and they sat in silence for what felt like a long time. "Look, Mom," she began.

"I'm sorry about last night." They stared at each other for a moment after nearly saying it in unison before laughing.

"I didn't mean to upset you with any of this," Tara went on.

"I know, love," said Mom. "I may not be happy about it, but I will try my best to support you. And I am genuinely proud of you. That scholarship is a great accomplishment. I guess I'm just having one of my 'Mommy Moments.' You're growing up so quickly and you're my first baby. I'm really going to miss you. I don't want anything to happen to you."

"Things happening are a part of growing up," Tara said. "And, like Dad said, I'm only a couple of hours away."

"I know," said Mom. Tara noticed her mom shudder and wouldn't meet her gaze. "It's still a big step." She stood. "I need to go for a shower. Dad is making a bigger than usual family breakfast, so why don't you go give him a hand once you're dressed?"

They hugged one more time. Mom gave her an extra squeeze this time. Tara grabbed the only pair of shorts and t-shirt that wasn't packed, ran a brush through her long red hair, and pulled it up into a ponytail. She did a quick once over in the mirror, cringed at her not so flattering outfit, and headed downstairs.

Christine sat at the table, clutching her mug. Her head bobbed as she fought the need to sleep. Her eyes were heavy, and she just glared at everyone as she slowly sipped her coffee.

Dad flipped pancakes, fried eggs and bacon, and sang along to the country station on the radio. The mixture of the music and the sound of food sizzling on the griddle was a weekend tradition. Tara smiled. While Christine and Mom would listen if it was on, Tara shared her father's love of country music. Sometimes they would go for a drive, turn on their favorite station or a playlist, and just have an all-out in-car karaoke session.

Tara inhaled deeply as she pulled out her favorite coffee creamer. "Smells amazing, as per usual," she said. "I better get a gym membership. A summer on Gran's cooking, I won't fit in any of my clothes when school starts."

Dad chuckled. "I'm sure you'll be fine. She'll keep you busy at work. You'll be plenty active." He didn't completely look up as he switched between pans. "Is everything okay? I heard screaming. Your sister wouldn't tell me."

Tara paused slightly as she grabbed her mug of coffee. "I had a weird dream and was crying out in my sleep."

"What was it about?" This time, he looked up.

"Well... I don't—really remember," Tara said quickly as Mom came into the room.

Dad just nodded and remained silent. He knew to avoid pressing the situation to not end the morning with another argument like last night. When she set her mug down, he handed her a platter piled high with fresh pancakes. "Make yourself useful, kiddo."

Tara set the food on the table and took out plates and silverware. Mom grabbed the syrup, butter and poured herself some tea before helping to bring the rest of the food to the table. The mood was the complete opposite of the night before. Tara ate in silence for a while, enjoying her dad's stories about growing up in Coolersville.

"I heard someone might buy the old abandoned house in Old Town," he said. "That super spooky looking one on the hill. We used to dare each other to go inside the caves before they blocked it off. Kinda sad. We'd find bats. If you shined your flashlight just right, they'd all go flying out. My sisters would always shriek and run. My dad built bat houses and had them hanging all over the yard after the caves were sealed. Some of the best summers with hardly any mosquitoes."

"Why would they be afraid of bats?" Christine asked. "Bats are amazing."

Dad shrugged. "They thought they were spooky or something, I guess? Never thought to ask. Aideen said they were just flying rats."

Christine groaned. "She and I need to have a chat."

When everyone was full and the dishes were cleared, Tara did a final check of her list. She laughed when Christine made a face after Tara peeked into her closet. "I'm just making sure I have everything that's mine," she said.

"Everything I want, I took from your donation bags," Christine said. She crossed her arms and pretended to look offended. "I'm not the only one who steals your clothes."

Mom held up her hands. "Don't look at me. I got what I wanted from the donation bags, too."

"Must be nice," said Tara. "I'm bigger than both of you, so can't fit any of your stuff. I can't borrow back."

With everything set, it was time for goodbyes. Everyone went outside. Tara hugged her sister and then her parents. Mom held on for a bit longer.

"Please be careful there," she said. "I'm trying to be Supportive Mom like you want me to be but that doesn't remove my worry."

"Can you tell me why you're worried?" Tara asked.

Mom opened her mouth as if to say something, but stopped herself and shook her head. "Not right now. It's a lot, and you wanted to be on the road. I'll explain one day."

Tara wanted to push more, but Mom looked on the edge of tears. Dad picked up on this, too. He put his arms around his wife and kissed her forehead as Tara got into the car.

"Don't mess with your phone while driving," said Mom.

Tara tapped the GPS device on her dashboard. "That's why I borrowed this." She held up her purse to show her phone tucked away and set it on the passenger seat.

"Still, please just be careful," said Mom.

"I will," said Tara.

"Do you have enough gas?"

"I filled up yesterday."

"Wiper fluid?"

"Topped it off while at the gas station."

"How's your oil - okay?"

"I had an oil change and complete look over last week with the mechanic you recommended."

Finally, Dad chimed in. "Just call us when you get there."

"I will," said Tara. "Can I go now?"

"Yes," said Mom. "We love you." She leaned her head against her husband's shoulder.

"I love you, too," Tara said as she started her car. She backed out and waved.

She pulled out of the driveway and kept glancing in the rearview mirror until she couldn't see her family waving at her. This was finally the point of no return. She turned on her driving playlist, aptly titled "Freedom" and belted along. She was off to the next chapter in her life. She couldn't quite shake the feeling that this was going to be a wild ride. But she was ready... maybe.

He turned off the screen as darkness swallowed the room. The curtains were drawn in the large study so he could have a clear image. He always had ways of seeing things, one of the many perks of being who and what he was. And he had a particular interest in this girl for some reason.

But, as he watched the last day progress, he wondered if what he had heard was wrong. This girl had no power. She wasn't even a threat. He chuckled to himself, like anyone was really a threat to him. There was just something vaguely familiar about her.

And then there was that dream. He had watched it with her. It was interesting, if nothing else. But nothing that signified anything he should be worried about.

A soft sigh diverted his attention. He turned as someone called his name in a sing-song melodic voice.

"Darien... Darien..."

He smiled when he faced the mirror and she slowly appeared. She wore a low-cut, black gown that seemed to highlight the curves of her body. Her dark hair was loose and flowing. But she looked paler today. He wished he could reach out to her, touch her, just to even hold her, but she was a ghost, trapped in between worlds.

"You really should be resting," he said softly.

"Is she coming?" she asked.

"Yes, she just left," he said. "I don't know why you're concerned about her. She's ordinary."

"But, she's not," she said. Her eyes darkened and her voice sounded barely above a whisper. "She... just doesn't know... it yet. You've forgotten who her family is."

He raised an eyebrow. "Are you sure, my love? I know your premonitions are rarely wrong, but I think this might be one of those times."

Her eyes returned to their normal color as she pouted and fiddled with the crystal on a chain around her neck. "I don't want anyone to ruin our new toys. Do you really think this will help me for good this time? We've tried for so long and I'm so tired."

His chest ached as she pulled a shawl around her and let out a little whimper. "I know, my darling. I know. Nothing will get in our way this time. When you're free and well, we will have our run of this town and more." His voice was forceful in the intention behind it.

She continued to pout. "I'm tired of being here."

"You'll be out soon," he said. "I promise."

She toyed with the delicate lace on her dress. "Can we go to Paris for a while?"

He smiled. "Sure. That will be the first thing on our celebration list when you're better."

She blew him a kiss and then faded away. He sighed and walked out of the room.

CHAPTER 3

Tara arrived in Coolersville in the late morning. She had taken this trip a number of times with her family, but driving alone was a different feeling. She kept herself entertained with her extensive music playlist, imagined being a Broadway star belting out her favorite songs. She sipped on a large iced coffee to keep fueled in the summer heat. It was still a long drive, and she was glad to soon be out of the car.

Gran lived in an area known as Old Town. Almost all Victorian era or older homes, immaculately maintained by their owners and passed through the generations. Gran's house had been in Granddad's family and was their wedding gift. It was big, painted robin egg blue, with a huge wrap-around porch and a large yard with lots of garden space. Six bedrooms, three bathrooms, a huge kitchen, dining room, office, and living room, perfect for a family with five children.

Gran loved hosting parties and always tried to get all the kids and grandkids together. It rarely worked out. Everyone was scattered across the country and then there was Tara's mom's resistance when it came to anything to do with her in-laws.

Tara smiled as she pulled in. Balloons tied to rocks lining the driveway. A large banner hung on the porch reading "Welcome home" with Gran standing under it, beaming and waving. She was a petite, curvy woman with gray hair pulled into a bun and bright green eyes, several shades lighter than Tara's. Today she wore a floral blouse, black pants, and white sneakers.

Gran was down the stairs before the engine was off. She pulled Tara into a hug as soon as she was out of the car. "Oh, my sweetheart!" she exclaimed. "I've missed you so much!"

"Hi, Gran," Tara said, breathing her in. Gran always smelled of herbs and flowers. She worked in her large garden and made all sorts of things with what she grew, so the scent just seemed to cling to her—sweet and earthy.

"Well, let's not waste any time," Gran said as she started grabbing suitcases. "I'll help you unload, and then I need to run some errands. You can explore the house and do whatever you like while I'm gone."

"What do you have to do?" Tara asked as they headed into the house.

"Lorraine's been wanting a visit," Gran explained. "And I have a few odds and ends to do in town. I'll show you your room and you can organize as you please. Just make yourself at home until I get back. I made you some of your favorite chocolate chip cookies as a snack for while you unpack."

They finished unloading the car. Most of Tara's belongings were piled near the stairs. Gran led Tara upstairs and down the hall to show her the room. It used to belong to Nessa, Gran's youngest daughter. The walls were a pale lavender with a large canopy bed and hand built furniture. Tara ran her hand along the rolltop desk and eyed the large shelf waiting to be filled with books.

"What do you think?" Gran asked. "I repainted the walls and fixed up the furniture. They took a beating when Nessa lived here, but they should still hold up."

"I love it!" Tara exclaimed. She belly flopped onto the mattress and sighed when she felt how soft it was. "It's like laying on a cloud!"

Gran chuckled. "I'm glad. I'm going to head out now—so make yourself at home. And don't snoop... too much," she said playfully.

When Gran left to run her errands, Tara called home to let them know she made it okay. Then she decided to take Gran's advice and explore the house. She usually only saw the kitchen, dining room, living room, and first floor bathroom whenever she visited with her parents.

She decided to wander the second floor and work her way down. She moved some more things upstairs and unpacked a few essentials before glancing into all the bedrooms, still kept ready for guests with the little reminders of who used to be there. Her dad's trophy case, the vanity in Aunt Aideen's room with pictures from high school taped around it, a whole wall covered in travel postcards collected by Uncle Malcolm. On Gran's dresser, there was a candle almost burned down and a photo of Tara's granddad smiling at their 50th anniversary party.

When she was done, and spent a little more time unpacking, she came back to the first floor and went directly to Gran's office and library. The room took her breath away. Every wall was lined with shelves, unless there was a window. All the shelves were packed tight with books on all kinds of topics. There was a big desk with a computer and file cabinets on either side where Gran did the paperwork needed to manage her gift shop in town. Just behind the desk, there was an old police scanner on a wooden stand.

In a far corner, there was a stack of bean bag chairs. Tara pulled out one and plopped onto it. She just stared around the room, taking in every detail she could. The room smelled like old books and herbal tea. A faint buzzing came from the large computer on the desk. She started browsing the shelves.

Gran had books on everything. Classic literature, business, medicine, history, sports, well worn copies of children's literature, and an entire bookcase with steamy romance. As she wandered, occasionally flipping through a book that caught her interest, she came across one that looked out of place. It was old. A black leather cover with faded silver lettering on the spine that read "The Codex."

"Why would Gran have a book like this?" Tara wondered aloud. She tried to take it down to have a better look, but it barely moved. When she let go, she heard a series of clicks behind the wall. She jumped back with a small yelp as the bookcase moved forward and shifted to the side to reveal a staircase.

"I have the coolest grandmother ever!" Tara exclaimed. She danced in place. There was an actual secret passage! This was something out of a book.

She searched through the desk for a flashlight so she didn't drain her phone's battery and headed down. At the bottom, there was a short hallway. It looked like it was part of the basement, but redesigned for another purpose. There were a few lamps on the wall, so Tara slid the flashlight into her back pocket.

At the end of the hall was a large, ornate door, stained a deep brown with what Tara believed was a kind of Celtic knot pattern around the edge. She pushed the handle and discovered it wasn't locked. Slowly, she peeked inside.

The room was lit with similar lamps as in the hall. It looked like another library, but the things here were strange. There was a slight musty smell that all basements had, but nothing too overpowering or unbearable. Shelves were still packed with books but they looked much older. And there were also jars and bottles with oils and herbs. Dried flowers, lavender, rosebuds, and baby's breath that she recognized among others, hung on one wall. A notebook and pen sat on a table with an old chair.

In the center, there was a pedestal with a large book. Like the Codex, it had a worn black cover and silver faded lettering, but in a language Tara didn't understand. The edges of the pages were yellowed. She carefully opened it to see the writing and images as bright as the day they were printed. Tara still couldn't read the language, but she looked at the drawings and tried to take in every detail.

One image in particular struck her. A group of women in simple dresses dancing around a large bonfire with blue flames. *Like my dream,* Tara thought. But it couldn't be. Why would she dream about something she had never seen before? She turned another page, and the text began to glow. Softly at first, and then brighter and brighter.

Tara stepped back and shielded her eyes. When she did, images flashed through her mind. The scene from her dream but from a different perspective of one of the women trying to escape and protect others. A young woman screaming from labor pains as an older woman prepared herbs and sang to her. An old woman turning over what looked like tarot cards for someone dressed like they were in a position of power. A woman waving a hand over a crystal ball calling to those beyond this world in a seance. A younger Gran, with her daughters Aideen and Nessa, gathered around her as she performed some kind of ritual. Then... Gran and Tara's mother arguing. She couldn't hear the words, but she saw her mother pointing and the anger in her eyes while Gran looked ready to burst into tears.

The images vanished as quickly as they had arrived. The book returned to normal. Tara swayed backwards and fell to the floor, unconscious.

CHAPTER 4

WHEN TARA OPENED HER EYES, SHE WAS LYING ON THE couch. Something cold dripped down her neck. She reached up and felt a cold, damp cloth on her forehead. Slowly, details swam into focus. The big window with deep purple curtains, a wooden coffee table, bookshelves, a television, fireplace, loveseat, and chair. The smell was sweet and floral... familiar. She was in Gran's living room.

Tara sat up and saw she was not alone. Gran sat at her feet on the couch. Sitting in the big chair, a young woman about Tara's age. She had long, dark hair, tanned skin, and bright blue eyes.

"Who..."

"Hi, I'm Marissa," the girl said before Tara finished her question. "I work for your Gran. I wanted to meet you. I'm sorry if this is kind of awkward."

"What happened?" Tara asked. "How did I end up here?" She remembered the secret passage, the room in the basement, the book... the visions. "Gran, why do you have a freaking secret passage and spell books in your house?" She blurted out before she could stop her mouth from moving faster than her brain.

Gran took a deep breath. Her voice was calm as she poured tea from the little pot on the coffee table. She handed Tara a cup. Marissa crossed her legs in the big chair like an excited child waiting for story time.

"As much as I've been waiting for this conversation, I've been dreading it as well," Gran began.

"That doesn't make me feel better," said Tara.

Gran shook her head and chuckled. "I'm sorry, love. Tell me what happened, and I'll fill in any questions you may have."

"We're going to need more than just tea," Tara said. She took a deep breath and told them how she found the secret passage and the visions. "What was all that? What were you and Mom arguing about?"

"Something she has tried to keep you from your whole life," said Gran.

"My mom has never kept anything from us," Tara said.

"Oh, no?" Gran asked. "Haven't you ever wondered why she's so distant from me? Haven't you ever wondered why she fights so hard to stay away from this town?"

Tara nodded. That was a big part of the argument last night. Tara wanted answers and wanted her mother's support.

"So, what is this secret?" Tara asked. "And, does Dad know?"

"Of course he knows," said Gran. "He's also wanted to share this with you girls. You are descended from a long line of witches."

"Witches?" Tara repeated. "Like green, pointy hats, warts, cackling on a broomstick? Or Buffy and Charmed?"

"Definitely more like Charmed, bad ass and powerful." said Marissa.

"So, is the secret passage part of the basement?" Tara asked.

"Yes, your Granddad added it after we moved here," said Gran. "He basically walled off half the basement. I wanted a place to be tucked away. I don't broadcast this information. Narrow minds and all." She said, tapped her finger against her head.

"Uh huh…" Tara managed. Her mother immediately came to mind as one of those people. She glanced at Marissa. "Clearly you're in on the secret."

"Oh yeah," said Marissa. "I'm also a witch. It's a little different in my family. While for you, it's mostly through the women in Gran's line. Magic is a bit more random for me. Like generational clumps. But it's one of the things our grandmas bonded over as kids."

Tara rubbed her temples. "I have so many questions." She clutched her stomach as she felt a familiar growl. "And, apparently hungry."

"Tell you what," said Gran. "Drink your tea and try to recover a bit. You had a big shock, so I don't think you're up for going out." Tara shook her head. "I have plenty of things here to make a nice meal for us and, between Marissa and I, we'll try to answer all your questions."

Tara nodded. "That sounds like a good plan." She sipped at her tea while she stretched out on the couch and allowed herself to slowly drift off to sleep.

Tara woke to the wafting smell of spaghetti. She sat up and slowly braced for a headache, but she felt so much better. She swayed a little when she stood up, but quickly recovered and followed the tantalizing smell into the kitchen.

Marissa stood at the stove, stirring a pot of sauce. Gran sat at the little table, scooping out meatballs. She looked up and grinned. "Feeling any better?" She gestured to a chair and handed Tara a scoop.

Tara sat down and fell into her task. Her dad did the same thing at home when he wanted help cooking, so this felt familiar. "The nap and the tea definitely helped," she said. "My head is still spinning, trying to sort out all the questions in my brain."

"Well, ask the first thing that really comes to mind and we'll go from there," Gran suggested. "You already experienced some of my work with the tea. It's an old family recipe with a magical twist."

"That's why it worked so wonderfully," Tara said. She thought for a minute and smiled. There was only one question that had to go first. "Can I see? Can I see some more magic?"

Gran blinked for a moment, suddenly taken aback, but then let out the most delighted laugh. She clapped her hands together and then pulled her granddaughter into a hug. She pulled back, snapped her fingers, and the flame on the stove flashed.

"Hey!" Marissa exclaimed, leaping back. "How about you show off when I'm not standing nearby to get incinerated, huh? I've got hairspray in my hair... I'll light up like a Christmas tree." Marissa examined the ends of her hair. "Note to self, never do a hairstyle that requires hairspray when I come over here."

Gran laughed, and Tara smirked. "Sorry," said Gran. "Take a break for a bit and help us. Sooner we finish, sooner we can eat." Gran snapped her fingers again, and the spoon began stirring on its own.

Marissa grabbed a bottle of water from the refrigerator and it slowly glided through the air across the room. She grinned when Tara gaped at her. "Well, I figure since we're showing off. This one took practice," she said. "I can't tell you how many dishes I broke before I got it right."

"And, after your Nana made you practice on things less smashable," Gran teased.

Marissa shrugged. "Yeah, that, too." She smirked.

"It's amazing!" said Tara. "Why aren't you more open about it?"

Gran shrugged. "I prefer to use my skills in more subtle ways that help people," she explained. "Like my little teas and herb mixes. There is no rule against it. There are plenty who do. Some live here in town. There's apparently a small coven at the college. I just never saw a need to advertise my skills."

Tara turned to Marissa. "What about you?"

"Nah," said Marissa. "Never saw a use for it either. And my Nana is definitely against being a more open practitioner. Most people think we're weird hippie spiritualists or something and leave us be. There are too many nuts out there who will automatically judge and think we sacrifice babies and all that middle ages bull..."

"Ahem!" Gran crossed her arms.

"...malarkey..." Marissa finished, smirking. "Sorry, Ms. K."

Gran just nodded with a slight smile and placed the last meatball on the tray. She put it in the oven and everyone washed their hands. Tara continued to come up with questions.

"What do you use magic for?"

"Anything, really," said Marissa. "But it's not necessary all the time. Hence another reason it's not clear to the world. It would be exhausting."

"Like in some movies where they talk about magic having a cost," said Tara.

"Exactly," said Gran. "Little things like the flame and the water bottle, that takes a little energy. Over time, you build up endurance, like any kind of exercise. Larger things, like a big ritual, can take more. If you decide to make it rain, that can throw off weather patterns until Nature rights itself again."

"I read on a witch blog about a woman who was in debt and did a money spell to suddenly have cash," said Marissa. "Then, she found out her aunt, who was in the best of health, suddenly died and left her a large inheritance."

"Jeez!" Tara exclaimed. "That's awful."

"Yeah," said Marissa. "So, you gotta watch stuff like that."

"So, that is why you don't just do a spell to tend your garden or clean the house," said Tara. "The cost of doing that constantly is too much to be worth it."

"Yes," said Gran. "And I like tending my garden. I may send the duster flying around if I have a backache or something. I'm not as young as I once was. But, it's only in some cases. And don't you dare tell me I need to move to a senior apartment like your Aunt Aideen has been trying to get me to do!"

Tara and Marissa both held up their hands. "Wouldn't dream of it!" said Tara.

"Good," said Gran. "I may be in my... well, I'm up there enough. But, if I could handle having a baby in my 50s, I can live in this house at this stage in my life. My Granny lived to be 125 years old. My ma was nearly that. I have plenty of years left in me."

"Papa said witches live so long to spite the Inquisitors and witch hunters," said Marissa.

Gran laughed again. "Yes, your papa would say that, wouldn't he?" She went over to the stove and stopped the spoon from stirring. She tasted the sauce, thought for a minute, and then turned the heat off before getting out another pot for boiling pasta. "Do you have any other questions?" She asked as she filled the pot with water and a sprinkle of salt.

Tara thought for a moment. She had a ton. It was a matter of picking out the right one. "Did anyone ever not want to..." She paused, trying to figure out how to phrase it just right.

"Did anyone ever give it up?" Gran clarified. Tara nodded. "Yes, there are two that I have witnessed. My mother did. We never figured out a reason, but my father did not like it. She hoped he would come around, but he didn't. So, she went to my Granny, and they both cried while they performed the ritual."

"I could never do that," said Marissa. "Your magic is a part of you. And if someone wouldn't let me be all of my true self, I don't think I could be with that person."

"My father was a wonderful man," Gran said. "He passed away before he could join us here, so my Granny taught me and my sisters."

"Could they reverse the ritual if they decided they wanted to be magical again?" Tara asked.

"Sadly not, once the powers are stripped, that's it. It's like stripping away a part of you." said Gran. "But, my granny did share a lot of the traditions that didn't require magic and would give us tips on our spells."

They sat in silence for a minute before Tara asked, "Who was the other person?"

"Your mother," Gran said.

Tara nearly fell out of her seat. "What!"

"Yes, she grew up here," said Gran. "Her paternal grandmother, I believe, was a witch. I don't think it passes to every generation, but I can't be sure. Anyway, she will never admit to any of it."

"What happened?" Tara asked.

"When she was in college, it was discovered that something was draining on her strength," Gran explained. "She was very weak and her life was at dangerous risk. We couldn't find a cause. Not for a lack of trying. Something always seemed to block us. So, a group of us got together, and it was decided that we had to strip her power in order to save her life."

"Makes sense," said Marissa. "If you can't find the cause, but you need to stop it from happening."

"Yes," said Gran. "She was terrified, of course. It's very painful. We did the ritual and she began to recover. But she was traumatized from it and vowed that she would not go near anything magic or associate with other witches because they were too dangerous. She transferred schools, which broke your dad's heart. They had been friends since they were little and I think he had a crush on her for quite some time. And then her family moved away a couple of years later. She will not come here if she can help it."

"That makes sense now," said Tara. "It's crazy. I'm having a hard time believing it. But, it somehow makes sense. So, how did she and Dad get together? If you were one of the ones who performed the ritual or whatever, and growing up here, she knew he was your son."

"They stayed in touch after she left," Gran explained. "She didn't blame him for what happened, even though she came to despise me. He went to visit her a few times. They started dating. It took some convincing when he wanted to ask her to marry him. He agreed to go along with her rule of no magic because he loved her. She feels the way she does to protect you and Christine. And we've debated... well, honestly, just argued... for twenty years about it. She wanted to strip you and your sister of your potential abilities when you were young, but I flat out refused. Embracing magic or rejecting the magic has to be your decision... and your decision only. Don't let anyone complicate that. She'll say we did it without her consent but she agreed. She was just scared, which is completely understandable."

"He mentioned in passing how much fun they had in college," said Tara. "But she shut him down real fast. Now I understand why. "

The timer beeped on the oven and dinner prep continued with more small talk. Tara could see the sadness in Gran's eyes as she remembered those events. She decided to save more of her questions for later.

CHAPTER 5

After dinner, Tara went to the backyard with Marissa. "I don't think you should try today," she explained. "But, I can show you some basic stuff. We can call it Magic 101."

"I think I can handle it a little," said Tara. "I'm doing much better now that some time has passed and I've had a good meal and Gran's tea."

"Alright, if you're sure. Come stand next to me, then," Marissa instructed. "And let's make sure there's space between us and the house and the garden. I'd rather not have your Gran turn me into a ferret if I damaged her roses."

Tara did as she was told. The yard was large enough that there were at least a couple of yards around them of free space. The sky was a mix of pinks and purples as the sun started to set with an occasional blink from a firefly. The smell of Gran's garden surrounded them in the sweet, earthy scent of summer.

"A big part of magic is visualization," Marissa explained. "So, we'll start with some easy conjuring. Hold out your hand." Tara did as she was told. "Close your eyes and imagine a ball about the size of a baseball. But, it's made of snow. Feel the shape and the sensation of the cold on your skin. Maybe it crunches a bit if you squeeze it."

Tara focused and lost herself in Marissa's words, her voice almost coolly hypnotic as it echoed in her head. As she focused, the temperature in the surrounding air dropped. It no longer resembled a warm June evening. Goosebumps ran up and down her limbs and the wind rushed past her ears. She felt something form in her hands. When she opened her eyes, her jaw dropped.

"I did it!" she exclaimed, and *plop!* the snowball tumbled from her hands and melted away. "Crap."

"Not bad for a first try," said Marissa. "Let's try again. Fire is similar, but we're not going to risk igniting the garden. Ms. K will turn us into worms and use us for fish bait."

"Agreed," said Tara. She stretched her arms and rolled her shoulders. "Let's try this again. I won't drop it this time."

"Alright," said Marissa. "Hold out your hand. I'll do it with you this time." She stood in front of Tara and mirrored her. "Concentrate on the size of the ball, the temperature, the texture."

Tara closed her eyes and repeated, following Marissa's instructions. The temperature dropped, the wind picked up and swirled around them. Slowly this time, she opened her eyes and looked at the ice ball in her hands.

"You're a natural!" Marissa exclaimed, and she launched her snowball towards Tara.

"Hey!" Tara cried, just able to dodge and, once again, dropping hers.

Marissa laughed. "Sorry, couldn't help it. How did that feel this time around?"

"Well, it happened faster," said Tara. "It feels weird, but also right."

"You've got magic on both sides of your family," said Marissa. "That's helpful if you work on honing your power. Let's try it again."

After the third try, Tara's legs went weak. She stumbled to a chair, out of breath, her heart racing. "Is magic supposed to be this exhausting?"

"At first, yeah, it can be," said Marissa. "Remember when we talked about having a cost? Sometimes that is your energy. You've got to build your endurance. That comes with experience and practice, and then it's not such a rough feeling. You're also already tired from travel and everything else today."

Tara nodded. "Like starting an exercise regimen," Tara said. "The first couple times you go to the gym, you feel like death the next day, but you push through and build up your muscles and then it doesn't hurt as much." She poured herself some iced tea they had brought outside with them.

"Exactly." Marissa sat next to her and helped herself to a cookie. "How are you really handling all this new info?" Marissa asked.

"I'm still processing it," said Tara. "I mean, my mom was a part of this world that I've only read about in books or seen in movies. And she had it ripped away from her. Stripped from her, that must feel so violating."

"I agree. You should talk to her about it at some point," Marissa suggested.

"I know I should," Tara said. "I want to take some time and absorb all of this information first. And then figure out how to bring it up. It's not going to be a very pretty conversation."

"Maybe talk to your dad first," said Marissa. "He's familiar with both sides of the story. Maybe he can help you approach her about it."

Tara nodded and then yawned. "Alright, I think I've had enough excitement for today. Do you want to stay the night? I could use the help with some more unpacking before I finally go to bed."

"Sure," said Marissa. "I'd be happy to help you."

They went inside, carried a couple more boxes upstairs to Tara's room, and then helped themselves to more cookies.

"What about your family?" Tara asked. "I know about your grandmother."

Marissa didn't answer right away.

Tara turned red. "I'm sorry. If this is a touchy subject, you don't have to answer. You can tell me to back off."

"No, it's okay," Marissa said. She sat on the floor and took a bite of cookie. "It's just me and Nana. She's my mom's mom. My Dad died in a car wreck when I was 2 years old. Mom did not take it well. I don't know all the details of what she went through since I was so young. I know she had a hard time holding down a job. We had to move in with Nana and Papa."

"That's rough," said Tara. "I'm so sorry."

Marissa sent her a sad smile. "Thanks. I don't remember him much. Flashes of memories here and there. I know they were crazy in love. Sort of a Romeo and Juliet thing, except they ran away together instead of... well, you've read the play. His family didn't approve but he didn't care. Then, when I was 5, my mom took off one night."

"What?" Tara exclaimed.

"Yeah, I overheard her and Nana arguing late one night," Marissa said. "She grabbed her suitcase and walked out to a waiting car."

"Did your Nana ever say why?" Tara asked.

Marissa shook her head. "That is a touchy subject," she said. "To this day, she doesn't like to talk about it. She has promised me to tell all one day, but it's never the right time. And your gran was sworn to secrecy, so no point asking her instead."

"Understandable," said Tara. "Don't want to betray a friend's trust. Especially given how close they are."

"Oh yeah, I don't fault her at all," said Marissa. "It's been 13 years, though. I'd like some answers."

"Yep, can totally sympathize," said Tara. She paused and took a bite of cookie. "Hopefully now I'll get some of my questions answered."

"Absolutely," said Marissa.

Darien stood in the clearing in the middle of the woods, admiring the work he had done. As soon as the sun went down, he came to this spot. He had set up precautions, so he was not disturbed. His plan had to succeed. He worked for far too long for this. He didn't want to show it in front of her, but he was getting desperate. And when things were desperate, caution was thrown to the wind. Nothing was going to get in his way.

Her image floated gently before him. Beautiful Lilia. As she used to be. Strong, powerful, the queen of chaos. Able to bring nations to their knees. This was who he fell in love with so many years ago. The image shifted to the present day. Trapped, weakened, unable to cross over fully into this world. All because those witches got in the way years ago. He loved her still. And he wanted his revenge more with each passing day. But it scared him. He didn't want to lose her again. And, if this was what he had to do, so be it.

He snapped his fingers and the ring of candles licked with flames began igniting. His eyes flashed red, and he smiled. "It begins."

CHAPTER 6

"BEEP! BEEP! BEEP!" Tara's alarm blared early in the morning. She smacked the button to turn it off and pulled the covers over her head, only to have it yanked back. She squealed and covered herself.

"If you had gone to sleep at a decent hour, you wouldn't be so tired," she heard Gran say. "Come on now, get a move on. I'm making breakfast."

"Will there be coffee?" Tara groaned.

"Yes, with your favorite vanilla creamer. Now scoot!"

Tara sighed and dragged herself out of bed, careful not to step on Marissa, who just burrowed deeper into her sleeping bag. She grabbed her favorite jeans and a green blouse. She showered in a hurry, pulled her hair up into a braid, and went downstairs. The scent of scrambled eggs, French toast, and bacon filled the air.

A few minutes later, Marissa, dressed in a purple blouse and a miniskirt, joined them. She went right to the cabinet and pulled out the biggest cup she could find for her coffee. She plopped into a chair at the little table in the kitchen, took a long sip, sighed happily and then said, "Good morning, everyone."

Tara smiled. She thought of her sister, Christine, needing caffeine in the morning as she poured herself a large mug. Then she turned and said, "Gran, I do have a question - about the witchy stuff."

"What is it?" Gran asked as she turned the bacon crackling in the pan.

"I want to learn about all the witchy stuff, but I don't know if I want to stick with it or not," Tara said.

"I can give you some time if you like?" Gran suggested.

"Yeah, perfect," said Tara. "And I can figure out how to talk to Mom and Dad."

"You don't have to rush that," said Gran. "But, you don't have to decide anything until, let's say, the end of summer."

"Sounds like a plan," said Tara.

Marissa leaped to her feet and danced around the room. "We are going to have so much fun! Some might even say it will be magical." She smirked when she saw the look on Tara's face and sat back down. "What? I get excited easily. There are a few witches in town, but I'm only close to a small handful. And they're all much older than me."

When breakfast was done, the girls helped Gran with the dishes and they piled into the car to head to town. Gran showed Tara how to disarm the security system and their opening routine before unlocking the doors to the store. As they walked through everything, they heard music across the street. People were talking and laughing. It looked like a block party was being set up. Booths with games, food trucks, and the local college radio station were all clustered in front of a storefront with a large "Grand Opening" sign.

"Ooh! Is that today?" exclaimed Marissa.

"Is what today?" Tara asked.

"The jewelry store across the street is opening," explained Marissa. "Mr. Moon is finally opening his doors."

"I believe your father did know him in school," Gran said. "Very nice young man. Came here and lived with his uncle just before high school, I think. Maybe a little sooner. Older man, a bit of a recluse. I don't remember much about his parents, besides they were made of money and sent him some regularly. He would frequently help with any town projects. Went away to college and met his wife, Ruby. They married, settled down back here, and he'd been working for years to open this store."

"That's nice," said Tara.

"Also, he's gorgeous," said Marissa. "Kind of a shame he's married."

Gran just laughed and pulled Tara away from the window. "You can go check things out at lunch. Time to start on some store training."

Gran showed Tara how to work the cash register. Marissa wrote out a little cheat sheet to help her learn the codes to correctly ring in items. "Most of the day," Gran explained, "you'll just spend it tidying the shelves and restocking. When someone is here, you can take turns with whoever else is working, since we only have one register. I'm working on getting a couple of tablets so we can finally be rid of that obnoxiously loud outdated credit card machine. But it's not in the budget yet."

Almost as soon as the doors were unlocked, people showed up. Two things were happening in town. The new girl working at Cait's Gifts and Novelties, Gran's store, and the grand opening of the jewelry store. Both were new and exciting, so everyone turned out.

"What really goes on here–that I'm considered news?" Tara asked Marissa.

"Nothing," said Marissa. "So, this is huge."

The first person introduced to Tara was Shylah Singh. She owned the Apothecary down the road and was opening a little late so she could meet Tara. She was a beautiful Indian woman, tall, curves in all the right places. Her golden brown eyes stood out with her dark skin and long, silky black hair that reached her backside. "I have heard so much about you," she said. Her voice was soft, a luxurious soothing tone with a hint of an accent. "Be sure to stop by my shop if you want any books or to build up some of your supplies."

Tara looked at Gran, confused. "The Apothecary, is the only witchy place to get materials for spells and such," Gran explained. "Shylah is also a witch, although much more 'out of the broom closet' than we are."

"I also carry some books on religion, philosophy, and psychology," Shylah said. "Well, anything that sparks my interest, really. Anyway, I better get going to open my shop. See you all later."

Rose Owen, one of Gran's other employees, popped in to pick up her paycheck. She was a petite woman in her mid forties with medium brown skin and cropped brown hair with purple highlights. She shook Tara's hand. "Welcome. It will be so nice to have some extra help around here. I feel bad because my kids are in all kinds of activities, so my schedule is all over the place. But I love working here with Gran."

"When am I going to see my little pal?" Marissa asked with a little pout.

"I'll bring him by soon," said Rose. "He's been begging to come visit you too."

A while later, a woman came in with two preteen children. She had long, bleach blond hair and brown eyes. She was very slim, wore a tight pencil skirt, blouse, heels, and an expensive name brand purse swung over her shoulder. Her daughter was a near spitting image, right down to the sucking-on-lemons sour look on her face. The boy had darker hair but the same cold eyes and an impeccably styled outfit.

"Aw, shit," Marissa muttered. "It's the Tillmans." She dragged Tara into the office. Gran rolled her eyes and went to speak with them.

"Who are the Tillmans?" Tara asked as they peeked out of the cracked open door.

"Mrs. Anya Tillman is the 4th trophy wife, although longest lasting so far, of Dennis Tillman," Marissa began. "He's a councilman, a millionaire, and an egotistical, misogynistic human cat turd."

"Geez, tell me how you really feel," Tara teased. She gave Marissa a nudge on the arm.

Marissa just glared across the room. "I was trying to be mild," she said. "Her twin demon spawn, Denny, or Dennis Junior, and Scarlet, are like their parents. Entitled ass hats." They watched as Gran chatted with Mrs. Tillman, and the kids glanced around the shop in disgust. Scarlet walked over to a display of necklaces, pointed at them, and made a gagging motion, sending her brother into silent snickers. Marissa fumed. "See? Entitled ass hat. Doesn't appreciate art. Those necklaces are hand beaded."

"If this guy has been married 4 times, does he have other kids?" Tara asked.

"Oh yeah," said Marissa. "Dude's like 70 or something. And Anya is around forty."

"Gross!"

"Yup. In terms of offspring he acknowledges, he has a son the same age as, if not older than, Anya, and another daughter our age. She hates my guts. And the feeling's mutual. I may have made her croak like a frog in the second grade."

Tara snorted. "You what?"

Marissa grinned. "I'll tell you the story another time."

"Mother," they heard Scarlet say. Her voice was high pitched, almost grating, and whiny. "I want that." She pointed to a ceramic castle on a shelf.

"No," said Mrs. Tillman. She pulled her daughter in front of her and tidied her hair. "Not today, my angel. We have too much to do today. And you won't want to carry it around."

"But Mommy, I neeeed it for my collection!" the girl wailed.

"We can come back for it later," said Mrs. Tillman, rolling her eyes.

"Somebody will buy it before then." Scarlet shook herself from her mother and stood with her hands on hips. "I want it."

"I'd be happy to hold it for you," Gran said.

"Like hell," muttered Marissa. "Hold it, they don't come back. We lose a sale for the day. She does this all the time."

"Not necessary," said Mrs. Tillman. "Because it's not happening."

"You never get me anything I want!" Scarlet wailed.

Marissa raced out of the office and shouted but it was too late. Scarlet was at the main window display. With a shriek, she knocked everything over. Stands toppled, glass shattered with a loud crashing sound echoing through the store. Other customers stopped their browsing and stared at the scene. Even some people outside paused what they were doing.

Then, as if a switch had flipped, she stuck her nose in the air, turned, and walked out. Her mother and brother followed without a word. Tara watched them go and could hear the kids laughing as they walked away.

"They planned that!" Tara said, a shocked look on her face.

"Of course they did," said Marissa. She grabbed the broom and dustpan from the utility closet. "At least once a week they go somewhere, make a scene, maybe destroy something, and leave. And everyone's too scared to say anything because Daddy T will threaten to drive them out of business."

"Good Lord!"

Tara volunteered to clean up the shattered display in the window. Gran decided to showcase some less fragile items this time and left it up to Tara and Marissa to set it all up. As they worked, Tara glanced across the street at the people gathering at Mr. Moon's party. It wasn't long before lunch break and Tara was curious to see what was going on.

Two more people came into the store. One was a short, curvy woman with dark, curly hair and brown eyes. She was dressed plainly in jeans and a floral blouse and light makeup. The other person was tall, broad shouldered, with long, silvery hair. They wore a black bell-sleeve top that came to their knees, leggings, high heel boots with silver studs running along the sides. Pale makeup with a dark smoky eye and deep red lipstick.

The shorter woman introduced herself as Ms. Glory. She was the head librarian. "Your Gran says you love to write."

"Very much," said Tara.

"We just opened our writers center," said Ms. Glory. "Brand new addition to the library. Trying to get some speakers to come in and do conferences and seminars. I can drop off an events calendar if you like, once we get things set."

"I'd love that," said Tara, beaming.

The taller person stepped forward and held out their hand. "Hey there, I'm Charlotte," they said. Tara noticed a bit of a Southern accent. "I run Attitude. It's a night club near the college."

"Attitude is fantastic," said Marissa. "Drag shows and the best karaoke in town."

Charlotte laughed. "I think it's the only place with karaoke in town."

"Still," said Marissa. "I counted the days last October to my 18th birthday so I could get in!"

"Definitely will have to get my dad to go someday," Tara said. "He has a fantastic singing voice."

"Looking forward to seeing you," said Charlotte. "We'll let you get back to work. See you around!" The two friends walked off to browse and chat with Gran while the girls finished setting up the window.

Finally, it was time to take their lunch breaks. Gran inspected the display and, when it was granted her stamp of approval, the girls grabbed their purses and headed across the street.

It was a block party atmosphere. People mingled and danced to the music playing from the radio station booth. The smell of fried food filled the air. Tara's stomach rumbled. They stood in the crowd for the giveaway wheel that Mr. Moon ran himself.

"He's so gorgeous," Marissa swooned as they waited.

Mr. Moon was a very tall man with slicked back, dark hair. His skin was tanned and his eyes were an unusual light green, almost cat-like. He wore black pants and a light blue collared shirt. Tara figured he was at least in his late 50s, if not already 60, if he had gone to school with her parents, but he looked much younger.

"Step right up, step right up," he called. "Spin the wheel, win a prize."

"Why are you giving jewelry away?" someone asked.

"Well," said Mr. Moon, "I wanted to show my appreciation for all the support this town has given me over the years. And the warm welcome you've given my lovely wife." He gestured to the woman standing behind the case, holding the prizes. She blushed and waved as everyone applauded.

"She's pretty," Marissa said quietly to Tara. Mrs. Ruby Moon was easily a foot shorter than her husband. She had black hair tied into a bun, brown eyes, and a fair complexion. She wore a hot pink top and cropped jeans with cute black strappy sandals.

"She looks a little uncomfortable being put on the spot," Tara observed.

"What kind of stones are they?" Marissa asked when they neared the front of the line. She looked at the prize wheel and could see photos of the different pieces. "They look like emeralds."

"They often get confused for emeralds," said Mr. Moon. "They're actually a rare variation of garnet. Try your luck?"

Tara stepped forward and spun the wheel. It landed on a necklace with a heart-shaped pendant. "Ah, good choice," said Mr. Moon. His wife passed over a box from the pile.

Marissa's turn came next, and she won a pair of earrings.

Lunch was nearly half over, so they stopped at one of the food trucks and headed back to the store. As they reached the door, Tara stumbled as someone bumped into her. "Hey!"

"I'm so sorry!" said a male voice.

Tara turned and her face went red. She saw a young man about her age, tall, stocky, with wavy shoulder length hair and gray eyes. "No, it was my fault," she said, her voice suddenly breathless.

"Hiya, Henry," said Marissa. She stood aside as he walked into the store. She smirked at Tara, who shook her head and tried to act like she wasn't suddenly anxious and awkward.

"What's going on, Marissa?" Henry asked.

"The usual. I see you met my new coworker," said Marissa. "This is Tara. She just moved here."

"Why would you willingly move here?" Henry asked. He let out a chuckle.

"My grandma lives here," said Tara. She fiddled with the box in her hands. "She's Mrs. Kavanagh."

"Really? Very cool," said Henry. "Maybe you can help me, then. My aunt's birthday is today and I sort of kinda maybe forgot to get her a present."

"Sure," said Tara. "Let me set this stuff down." She put her purse, necklace, and lunch in Gran's office behind the front counter and returned to the floor. "What kind of things is your aunt interested in?"

"Weird crap," said Henry. "Tarot cards, ghosts, anything crazy like that. I know she would like something from the Apothecary but the smells in that place give me a serious headache."

"How about this?" She grabbed a book off the shelf.

"Historic Ghosts of Ohio volume 7," he read. "Perfect. I don't think she has this one yet."

"It just came out," said Tara. "I've been waiting for it myself. There are some interesting facts in there, along with super creepy ghost stories."

"Yeah, she has the rest of the series so this is perfect," said Henry. "Thanks so much."

He walked over to the counter as Tara rang him out. "How do you like it here?" he asked.

"I haven't had a chance to explore yet," said Tara. "It was like, arrive, start to settle in, and then start work."

"Yeah, that doesn't leave much time," said Henry.

When she handed him a receipt, he took a pen and wrote down his phone number. "Text me later, okay?"

"Yeah," Tara managed, as he walked out with his bag. They stood by the door and she added his number to her phone. "I'll do this now so you know it's me." She typed "Hi there. Tara" and hit send.

His phone dinged in his back pocket. "Great," he said. "See you around." Tara waved as he walked off.

Marissa, who was across the room, sent her a thumbs up and beamed at her.

About half an hour later, Rose burst in, calling for Gran to come help. Gran raced from her office. The screams from outside echoed into the store.

"What happened?"

"There were a few people who just passed out," Rose said. "One of them is Lydia from the Diner. She's pregnant. Shylah is on her way too, but she's going to need help until the paramedics arrive."

Gran pulled a first aid kit from behind the counter and followed Rose. Tara and Marissa stood near the door and watched. "Something doesn't feel right," said Marissa.

"What do you mean?" asked Tara.

"I can't quite place it," said Marissa. "But there's something weird going on."

The whistle of the ambulance siren came blaring down the street as the flashing lights danced against the faces of the crowd.

Tara breathed a sigh of relief as the paramedics pushed through the crowd. A few minutes later, five gurneys were being pushed back through. All five people on them were awake but looked dazed. Gran and Shylah came back into the shop and Gran leaned against the counter, a little worn down from whatever she had to do.

"Is everyone okay?" Tara asked. She pulled a chair out of the office. "Are you okay?"

"Yes, they should be fine," said Gran. She sat down, breathless. "I did a small recovery spell. It wasn't a lot, but I'm not as young as I once was, so it was all I could do for the number of people. I did a little more for Lydia because of her condition. They'll be under observation at the hospital and they'll figure out what happened, I'm sure. That took more out of me than I expected."

"What happened?" Marissa asked.

"They just... dropped," Gran said. Tara brought her a cup of coffee. "Out of nowhere, five people all at once. No connection between them, no medical history issues that I know of for any of them. And the only thing that worked was a revival spell."

Shylah handed Gran a piece of hard candy. "It's a new recipe I'm working on, it's green apple flavored" she said. "Let me know if it helps."

He watched as the crowd began to thin. How he managed to have enough concentration to do such a targeted spell, he'd never know. Maybe it was his sheer stubbornness. Maybe it was his desperation. But, it seemed to have the desired effect on the people. He hoped the end result was what he needed for her.

CHAPTER 7

Day two at Gran's store was a bit less eventful than Tara's first day at work had been. There were a few more people who came in to say hello, including Rose, with an update on the people taken to the hospital the day before.

"They couldn't figure out what was going on," said Rose. "So, everyone but Lydia was sent home this morning. No underlying health issues, nobody was dehydrated. They just… dropped."

"I'm telling you," said Marissa. "Something really feels – I dunno, off."

"Well, the Conspiracy Guy is having a field day with it," Rose said.

"Who's the Conspiracy Guy?" Tara asked.

"This nut I went to school with," Marissa explained. "Always recording things and then editing them in a way to sensationalize stories. He has a video channel and a blog and he's always posting stuff about how aliens built the pyramids and the moon landing was a staged event."

"Sounds like this guy needs a new mentally stable hobby," Tara said.

"Not going to happen," said Marissa. "He makes a hefty chunk through crowdfunding donations. Sadly, clickbait and fear mongering pays. He was even offered a sponsorship from a major propaganda cable network."

Toward lunch time, Gran asked the girls if they could run a few errands for her. "We're not too busy, so I can watch the store and it will be a way for Tara to introduce herself around town. And I have a surprise for the both of you."

She led them to the back stock room where two brand new bicycles sat. One was a bright purple with lavender and white streamers hanging from the handles. The other was green with green and blue streamers. Both bikes had little baskets on the front and back. "I figure you would need them for the school year, but I couldn't wait to give them to you."

"They're beautiful!" Tara exclaimed. She threw her arms around Gran in a big hug and laughed when Marissa did the same on the other side.

"Purple! Mine!" Marissa exclaimed. They snatched Gran's list, hopped on their bikes and headed out.

As they went around town, Marissa showed Tara some of her favorite places. They rode past the bookstore, called "Bookmark My Word." She also pointed out a few of her favorite restaurants and the coffee shop, called the Coffee Bunny Café, where she stopped nearly every day for "the best frozen mocha in the world."

By the end of the afternoon, Tara and Marissa had their arms full of bags, they were riding high on caffeine as they finished one of those mochas in the super jumbo size Marissa had insisted on, and they headed back down Main Street, laughing and telling more stories.

"So, tell me the story about making that girl croak," Tara said.

Marissa laughed. "In my defense, I was like 7 and not in full control of my power yet. Or my temper."

"Go on," Tara prodded.

"We were at school in music class," Marissa said. "The teacher wanted volunteers for a couple of solo songs for the school concert. She and I wanted the same song and neither would give in."

"I've known you for 3 days and this already does not surprise me," Tara teased.

Marissa smirked. "Yeah, it's a blessing and a curse, my stubbornness. Anyway, the teacher asked us both to sing and the class would vote."

"Nice democratic solution," said Tara.

"Except I'm a bad loser," said Marissa. "And I *definitely* was not going to lose to her! So, I sang the song and got some applause and praise from the class. She steps up, opens her mouth and *ribbit*."

Tara started cackling. "Just like that?"

"Just like that," said Marissa. "I don't know what I did besides stare daggers and silently wish it would happen. Apparently, for a volatile magical 2nd grader, that was enough. I thought it was hilarious. Went home and told

Nana and Papa about it. And then got grounded for two weeks."

Before she could react, Tara stopped sharply when her phone buzzed in her pocket. "It's my mom. She wants to video chat."

Marissa pointed to a bench nearby. "Let's rest and set our stuff down so you can talk easier."

As they propped their bikes against a wall, Tara swiped her screen to answer. "Hey, Mom. Hold on a sec." She arranged her bags so they didn't fall out of the basket and hung some on the handles. Then held the phone so she could be seen better without sun glare. "What's going on?"

"You didn't text me this morning," Mom said.

"Oh, sorry," said Tara, wincing. "Marissa and I were having a day out. Doing errands for Gran" She held up one of her bags and Marissa poked her head into view of the screen.

"Hi, Mrs. Tara's Mom!" Marissa said, shielding her eyes from the glare of the sun on the screen.

"Oh, that's..." Mom paused and squinted at the screen. "What is that building behind you?"

Tara glanced back to see they were in front of the Apothecary. "Oh, that's just..."

"That's that witchy store with all the herbs and oils and crazy crap, isn't it?" Mom demanded.

"I wouldn't know," Tara stammered. "I've..."

"Come home."

"What? Mom – come on."

"Did I stutter?" Mom snapped. "Tara Elizabeth, pack your bags and come home now. I will come down there and drag you home."

"What? Mom, no! I've only been here a couple of days."

"I don't want you anywhere near a store like that. I just knew you being down there was going to be a bad influence."

"I'm just sitting on a bench outside," Tara argued.

"I don't really care. You're coming home."

Mom was shouting now. Tara could hear her father in the background. "What's going on?"

"Liam, Tara needs to come home," Mom said off screen.

"Why? What's wrong?" Seeing Tara, he peeked over his wife's shoulder into view of the camera. "Hi, Pumpkin. Everything okay?"

"Yeah, hi, Daddy. I was just running errands for Gran with my friend."

"She went inside that witchy place!" Mom cried. "Look at where she's sitting."

"We were running errands for Gran and happened to be passing here when you called," Tara repeated. "We didn't go inside the store. I don't know why Mom is totally losing her mind."

"Alright, sweetie, don't worry," said Mr. Kavanagh. "Don't worry about it."

"What?!" Mom cried off screen.

"Michelle, cool it!" Dad said, his voice slightly raised. He turned back to his daughter. "You have fun, sweetie. I'll calm your mom down."

"Bye."

"No. Wait, Tara..." Dad ended the call before his wife could continue to argue.

Tara sighed and slumped on the bench. She rubbed her temples with her fingertips. "Oh, my God!"

"Wow!" was all Marissa could say.

"That was... well, humiliating," said Tara. "She saw just the sign for the Apothecary and freaked the hell out!"

"Not an uncommon response from people, even for someone who didn't go through what your mom did," said Marissa. "When Shy first opened, there were actual protests."

"What?"

"Yeah. Some group calling themselves 'The Purists' gathered and protested for like 2 weeks. It ended when one of them broke her windows. That's when the Mayor stepped in. Of course, they tried to sue the city, claiming a violation of free speech. But, the ruling was where the violence and destruction of public property begins, the line is drawn."

"Absolutely," said Tara. "What was the result?"

"The group was banned from the town and had to pay for all the damages," Marissa explained. "But enough about that. I'm starved. There's a Chinese place about a block from work. Let's get food and head back to the house."

"Sounds good," said Tara. "I'll call Gran and see what she wants. How about a musical movie marathon?"

"Yes, please!"

As they waited for their food, Tara's phone rang again. She smiled this time when she saw the name.

"Hello?"

"Tara? This is Henry. I got the right number?"

"Yeah, hey, how are you?" She stepped out of the restaurant and leaned against a wall.

"I'm okay. Listen, I was wondering what you're doing Friday night."

"Nothing except work and maybe some more unpacking, why?"

"Would you like to go out and get dinner with me? I can meet you after work."

"Sure, I'd like that. I'm done at 5:00."

"Cool. See you Friday."

Tara hung up just as Marissa came outside. "I just ordered. It'll be a few minutes. Is everything okay?"

"Henry just asked me to dinner," Tara said. She couldn't believe it even as she said it aloud.

"That's awesome," said Marissa. "He's really great."

"I'm a little nervous. Never been on a date before," said Tara as they walked back inside to wait for their order.

"Don't sweat it," said Marissa. "It's just dinner. Just go and have fun. Get to know each other."

CHAPTER 8

Darien sat in a darkened room, surrounded by black taper candles. He held a crystal in his hands and chanted in an ancient language long ago lost to humans. But he wasn't human. He despised most humans... pathetic emotional creatures. He merely looked like one and had lived among them long enough to seamlessly blend in.

He envisioned his target. The red-haired girl. He saw her going about her day and waited for the right time to strike.

Just after 5:00, Henry arrived at the shop. They walked a few blocks to a restaurant called the Amaryllis Steakhouse. Tara hesitated. She looked down at her denim shorts and blouse and felt very underdressed. The nicest thing she had was the necklace she won at Mr. Moon's opener.

Henry took her hand and smiled. "It's okay," he said. "This place looks fancy, but they're really cool."

They went inside and got a table tucked away in a corner. It was nicely decorated. It wasn't brightly lit, but it wasn't so dim that it was hard to see. Somehow, they reached a nice medium. Each table had a little bowl with a tea light inside surrounded by artificial flowers. Soft instrumental music played over speakers at various points in the room. A large bar with tall tables and stools took up about a quarter of the room. The rest were regular tables and booths with deep red cushions.

After they ordered and received their drinks, Henry asked, "So, how is your first week going?"

"Not too bad," said Tara. "My mom flipped out on me." She told him about the video call in front of the Apothecary and her mother's reaction.

"That's... pretty dramatic," Henry said.

Tara laughed. "I know. I mean, Shylah seems really sweet. And, I may go in and browse one day. But my mom went through some stuff when she was younger, so anything connected to places like that freak her out."

"She wouldn't get along with my aunt, then," said Henry. "Aunt Sally's into all that weird stuff. I guess she's considered a dabbler?" He shrugged and sipped his iced tea. "I know she's been meaning to go see Shylah, but she's been busy at the hospital. She's an Emergency Room nurse."

"Wow, yeah, she would be busy," said Tara. "What about the rest of your family?"

"Dad's not in the picture," said Henry. "So, Aunt Sally and my cousin, Katrin, moved in with me and Mom. Sally has a son,

Paul. They're the closest I have to siblings. Aside from my bandmates."

Tara perked up. "You're in a band? What are you called?"

"You promise you won't laugh?" Henry asked.

"I promise," said Tara. She held her hand up in a Girl Scout style salute.

"We're called the Nightwalkers."

"Ooh, I like it," said Tara. "Sounds spooky."

"Yeah, we do that on occasion," Henry explained. "Kai, he's the lead singer, gets in these 'inspired phases' where he comes up with original work. Mostly we do covers of rock and blues."

"What do you play?"

"Electric bass guitar," Henry said. He paused as the waitress delivered their food and thanked her. "I'm going to be in a jazz band in college. So, I've been taking some lessons for the double bass."

"That's the big one," said Tara. She gestured the height.

Henry nodded. "Yep. We had a different name in high school. Marissa and another girl sang with us. Sometimes doing backup vocals for Kai, sometimes we'd highlight them. Marissa is a fabulous singer. But, that didn't last."

"What happened?"

"The other girl, Gina, was a massive diva," Henry explained. "She'd get pissy if she wasn't the star of the show and we all had enough."

"That sounds rough," said Tara. "Why didn't you keep going just with Marissa?"

"That was the plan and then her grandma got sick so family took priority," said Henry. "I can totally respect that, though. And, we keep an open invite to join us whenever she wants. Do you play anything?"

"Nope," said Tara with a small laugh. "I was in choir in middle school and high school. And I was an extra in the school musicals every year. I didn't mind, though. A bigger part would have been fun, but I have some anxiety and it likes to rear its ugly head at the most inopportune times."

"Oof, that sucks," said Henry, as he took a bite of food. "What kind of music do you like?"

"Just about anything, really," said Tara. She pulled her old MP3 player from her purse that she had since she was a kid and refused to get rid of. She scrolled through her driving playlist. There was country, pop, rock, Broadway musicals, and even a bit of rap.

"Wow, that's a wide range," Henry commented. "What are you thinking of studying in college?"

Tara hesitated. "Well... you tell me first."

"Music education," he said right away.

"I actually don't know what I want to study yet," Tara confessed. She fiddled with the napkin on the table. "I applied to Continental, somehow got a full scholarship, which is wild, but I don't know. I have so many interests, but making a career out of those interests is another thing."

"You had to declare something, though, when you signed up for classes," Henry said.

Tara nodded. "I'm starting with journalism. I love to write. Concentrating on my basics and then I'll go from there."

He nodded, yawning and shook his head. "Oh man. I'm sorry."

"Oh, I can't be that boring, can I?"

"No, I..." he yawned again. "I'm not feeling quite right. Getting a bit of a headache."

Tara yawned next, and her stomach felt a little queasy. "Yeah, me, too. This is weird. I think we should go home."

"Want me to drive you back?" he asked, rubbing his head. He called over the waitress and asked for to-go boxes.

"No, I can make it to the shop and call Gran. Are you okay to drive?"

"If my headache continues, I can crash at a buddy's down the street," Henry said. They both yawned again. "Sorry, we have to cut this short. I was having a really good time."

Tara smiled. "Me, too." When they packed up their half-eaten meals, they got to their feet, paid the bill, and left the restaurant in separate directions.

Tara struggled to stay upright as she walked. Her vision blurred a little, and she saw little black squiggles floating in front of her. Squinting her eyes, trying to refocus her vision. Her queasy stomach increased as the headache formed. She forced herself to stop and lean against a brick wall of some sort of building. But when she stepped away, her legs turned to jelly, and she collapsed.

When she opened her eyes, she was lying on a couch. But it wasn't like on Monday when she was in Gran's living room. She was in a small office. She almost called out for Gran until she stopped to take in the details. She noticed the high quality furniture. The couch she was now sitting on was a deep brown leather and smelled new. There was also a top of the line computer on the decent size wooden desk behind her. Mrs. Moon entered the room with a tray, and Tara could hear voices just outside.

"Oh, good," Mrs. Moon said. "You're awake." She set the tray down and called outside. "Honey, our visitor - she's up."

Two people entered. Henry and "Mr. Moon?" Tara stared, shocked. She looked around and realized she must be in the office of the jewelry store.

"Hello, Tara," Mr. Moon said.

"What... how..." she asked, confusion flashing across her face.

"It's alright," said Mrs. Moon. "Take it easy." She helped Tara sit up slowly and gestured to the tray of tea and crackers. "I'm sorry this has to be our official introduction. Have something and we'll tell you everything."

Tara accepted the cup and sniffed. "Is that chamomile?"

Mrs. Moon nodded. "Yes, it's a good gentle restorative."

"I know," said Tara. "My Gran has an herb garden, and she's going to teach me this summer." She sipped again and sat back. The tea was warm, and she felt it soothing her throat as she swallowed. Her headache eased and her mind began to clear. It was like the first sip of coffee in the morning as her energy started to slowly return. "So... how did I end up here?"

"I started to feel better after I left the restaurant," Henry explained, taking a seat next to her. "But I didn't feel right about leaving you. I turned back and reached you just as you fell over. Mr. Moon happened to be locking up, so I flagged him down to give me a hand."

"Oh, no," Tara cried. "You were in view of my Gran's shop. Rose might have seen you."

"No," said Henry. "I saw her in there, but she was talking with a customer."

"I didn't want her to worry," said Mr. Moon. "So, I insisted you both come here."

"Yeah, I guess that makes sense. Gran's still going to be worried, though," said Tara. "How long was I out for?"

"A couple hours," said Henry. "I know, she's probably worried. I have five calls and 15 messages from my mom looking for me because it's past curfew. And it'll just be later by the time we get back to my car just off campus."

"I don't think I can walk that far yet," said Tara. She took another sip of tea.

"You're welcome to wait here while he goes to get his car," said Mr. Moon. "I'd drive you, but my car is in the shop. We were just finishing up paperwork for the day."

"How will you get home?" Tara asked.

"We have an apartment upstairs," Mr. Moon said. "It's fine."

Henry left to get his car while Tara sipped some more tea. "What a nice young man," Mrs. Moon commented. "How long have you been seeing each other?"

Tara turned bright red. "Tonight was our first time out. I just moved here this last week."

"Well, welcome to the town," said Mr. Moon, beaming. "I've been in and out of here for many years. Something always seems to draw me back."

"Do you remember my dad, Liam?" Tara asked. "My gran says she thought you went to school together. Liam Kavanagh."

Mr. Moon blinked. "Why, yes. That name is very familiar. We weren't best pals or anything like that. I think he let me cheat off a math test one time but we were acquainted. How is he doing?"

"Very well," Tara said. "He's a history teacher."

"Good for him," said Mr. Moon. "I sort of remember that was a subject he enjoyed."

"Yeah," said Tara. "The man is a walking encyclopedia of 20th century military history. My mom, Michelle, also grew up here. She left in the middle of college."

"Michelle Krasny?" Mr. Moon asked.

Tara nodded. "Yeah, that's her maiden name. You knew her, too?"

Mr. Moon chuckled. "We, uh... we dated for a while."

Mrs. Moon laughed. "What a small world."

"Isn't it just," said Mr. Moon.

Henry pulled up in front of the store. He helped Tara climb into his truck and she directed him to her house.

As he drove, she reached for Henry's hand and gave it a squeeze. "Thanks for sticking by me."

"What are friends for?" he said, squeezing her hand in return.

They pulled up to Kavanagh House just after 10:30. Tara sighed. Lights were still on. Gran was worrying. Before Henry put his truck in park, Gran was hurrying out of the house. Tara slid out and was immediately pulled into a hug.

"I had the worst feeling!" Gran cried. "Are you okay? What happened? Are you hurt?"

"I'm okay, Gran," she said. "Really, I am. Let me get into the house and I'll fill you in."

"What happened?" she asked. "Where's Henry? Did he...?"

Henry came around the front of the truck. "We're both fine," he said.

"I'll explain everything inside," Tara repeated.

"Well," said Gran. "I'm glad you're both okay." She turned to Henry. "And thank you for making sure she got home safe. Come and have some tea and a cookie, Henry."

"I'd love to but can't, Mrs. Kavanagh," said Henry. "My mom is on the edge of a meltdown already. I better get home and calm her down. I'll be seeing you." He waved at Tara and climbed back into the truck as Gran helped Tara into the house.

They made it to the living room and Tara needed to sit down. Her head was spinning again. Gran gave her a blanket and pillow. "Can you tell me what happened?"

"I don't really know," said Tara as she put her feet up and reclined, sinking into the big puffy pillows. She sighed as her body started to relax. "We were at dinner, having a nice time. The food was good and then we started to feel weird. I tried to walk back to the shop, but I passed out." She told Gran how Henry found her and Mr. Moon helped get her inside the jewelry shop's office.

"You're not going to make it upstairs," Gran noted. "Rest here. I'll see what I have in my remedy box to help you. And you should probably take a couple days off."

"What?" Tara sat up and immediately regretted it as a wave of nausea threatened to make her lose her dinner. She took some deep breaths and swallowed hard until the feeling faded. "I'm fine."

Gran raised an eyebrow. "It's just a precaution," she said.

Tara was too tired to argue, so she laid back, pulled the soft blanket over her and allowed the sleep to take her.

CHAPTER 9

For the next 2 days, all Tara could do was sleep on the couch. Gran stayed home from work to keep her hydrated and would wake her to give her some soup or a light sandwich. And then she would fall back to sleep.

By Monday, she started to feel a little better so she could be awake for short periods of time. She begged Gran to help her wash her hair in the kitchen sink. Her scalp felt like bugs were crawling on it with how much it itched.

In the afternoon, while sitting out on the front porch swing reading, Tara's phone rang. She tapped the screen to answer. "Hello?"

"Hey, Tara. It's Henry."

"Oh, hi!" She reclined back across the swing. "How are you?"

"I'm doing okay," he said. "I just wanted to make sure you were okay."

Tara beamed, and she felt her cheeks go hot. "I'm getting there," she said. "Slept a lot. But now able to be up a bit more."

"That's good," said Henry. "I heard a few more people have been admitted in the past couple of days with whatever this is."

"How do you know?" Tara asked.

"My aunt is an Emergency Room Nurse, remember?" he explained. "She's been working overtime all weekend. Dang near exhausted herself. Mom's worried she'll get whatever this is."

"Yikes," said Tara. "I hope they figure out what's going on."

"Conspiracy Guy is having a field day," said Henry. Tara could hear the annoyance in his voice.

"Marissa told me about him," Tara said. "What is with this guy?"

Henry chuckled. "I wish I knew. His real name is Allan James. We went to school together. He takes ordinary news, and writes sensationalized stories, sharing altered images on social media and his blog."

"Yeah, that's what Marissa said," said Tara. "She said he's got quite a following."

"Makes a killing, too," said Henry. "He just launched a line of merch with his most popular theories printed on things like t-shirts and bumper stickers and charges outrageous amounts. He said he has plans to come out with a supplement line to counteract "big pharma" or whatever. Aunt Sally was pissed when she heard that."

"I would, too," said Tara. She tried to say more but let out a big yawn.

"I'll let you rest," said Henry. "I'll talk to you later. I hope you feel better. I owe you a redo since the night was cut short."

Tara beamed. "I'd like that. Bye."

On Tuesday, Marissa came over to keep Tara company so Gran could return to work. They watched movies and Tara could stay awake for the most part. She did take a nap around lunch time.

When Gran returned home, Marissa ordered some pizza. As they ate and continued their movie marathon, Tara's phone rang. She glanced at it and turned it screen down.

"Who is calling you?" Gran asked.

Tara shrugged.

Gran sighed. She held out a hand and Tara's phone zipped across the room.

"Hey!" Tara exclaimed. She tried to grab it, but wasn't fast enough.

"You've been avoiding calls from your mother?" Gran scolded. She held up the phone and pointed to the 5 missed calls on the screen. And one angry face emoji text message.

"What am I supposed to say?" Tara demanded. "If I tell her the truth, she'll be down here before you can say bibbity bobbity boo, ready to stick me in a convent in Siberia or something."

"You may be overreacting just a bit," said Gran.

"No, I'm really not," said Tara. Gran glared, saying everything she needed to with just one look. "Alright, I'll call her, but I'm fudging details."

"Just so you call her, I don't care," said Gran. She tossed the phone back as it began to ring again. Tara took a deep breath and answered.

"Hi, Mom."

"Why haven't you answered? I've been worried sick."

"I've been busy with work and getting settled here," said Tara. "I don't always have my phone on me."

"Since when?" Mom asked. "It never left your hand at home."

"Did you need something?" Tara asked. "We're having dinner."

"I just wanted to make sure you're doing okay," said Mom.

"I'm fine. I'll talk to you later. I want to finish my dinner." She tapped the phone screen to end the call.

"You know that's just going to make things worse, right?" Gran asked.

"I'm too tired to care right now," said Tara, as she reached for another slice of pizza.

He returned one evening and immediately sensed something was wrong. He heard screaming and searched every room in the large house, trying to find the source. Finally, in one of the bedrooms, he saw her. Arms and head sticking out of the mirror but, beyond that, she couldn't move. Their gaze met, and she just started to sob.

"I thought I could do it!" she wailed. "I really thought I felt strong enough to break through... I'm not!"

He was across the room in a blink. He held onto the frame of the mirror and chanted. The surface rippled, and she was pulled backward. She dropped to her knees and continued to cry into her hands.

He hated seeing his beloved in such a state like that. It destroyed him. He despised being made to feel helpless and weak. He knelt so they could be at eye level. He touched the mirror, and she reached out her hand to meet his. "I'm sorry, my beloved" he said. "I'll keep trying."

He realized smaller attempts weren't going to be enough. He had to step things up. He went downstairs to his study, slammed his door in anger, losing himself in his books and research notes.

Tara managed to make it up to her room by mid-week and actually slept in her own room on Wednesday night. When she woke Thursday morning, she was feeling nearly normal.

"Can I please go back to work tomorrow?" she begged. "I'm tired of being cooped up in this house."

"Yes," said Gran. "If you're feeling up to it. But, the minute you start to feel tired again, you're coming back to rest."

"Sounds like a very good deal," Tara said.

"I mean it, Tara. And, since you're feeling better," Gran said, "I want to show you something." She led Tara to her office. Tara expected to go down into the spell room, but Gran slid back a small door on a shorter bookcase and pulled out a thick, well-worn book. Gran gestured to sit on the couch together in the living room.

The book had a brown leather cover with embossed images of tree branches. "This book has been passed down through at least 4 generations," Gran explained. "It's the chronicle of the women who inherited the magical skill." She flipped through some of the pages, searching for just the right place.

She pointed to a faded sepia tone photo of a middle age woman. She wore a Victorian style dress and looked off in the distance with a hint of a smile on her face. Similar facial features to Gran, Tara imagined the same fiery red hair that ran strong in that line of the family. "This is my Granny Lora," Gran explained. "She taught me almost everything I know. Absolutely brilliant and ahead of her time. She worked for the Suffrage movement in Scotland and all over the UK. I think I still have one of her badges somewhere. It said something like 'Witches for Women's Rights.'"

"That's fantastic," said Tara. Gran passed her the book, and she skimmed through, looking for something of interest. She came across a sketch of two girls holding hands.

"Ah, Brigid and Madeline," said Gran. "They lived in the 1550s, I think?"

"It says Brigid was born in 1535 and Madeline in 1540," Tara said, pointing to the text.

"Yes, I was close enough. Memory isn't as sharp as it used to be," Gran said. "Anyway, their parents died during a plague outbreak, so they had to make their way on their own. Brigid had her hands full. Madeline was adventurous and always getting into trouble. She liked to experiment with spells. And, of course, that was illegal at the time, so they had to be extremely careful."

"What happened?" Tara asked.

"They did manage to live long lives," said Gran. "Madeline did not have children of her own. But she wasn't one who could settle. I think I know where your Uncle Malcolm gets his love of traveling from. She did have many loves, but according to one story, they couldn't handle her personality and her wild untamed nature. Brigid did marry and had many children, 8 or 9 if I remember the stories. And, I believe Madeline came to live with them and they continued to practice in secret." She looked at her watch. "Goodness me, I need to get dinner going."

"Can I borrow this?" Tara asked.

"Of course," said Gran. She left Tara to keep reading.

Friday morning, he stood in the middle of the woods in a clearing. Thick, tall, black candles and an assortment of crystals were arranged in a circle around him. As he chanted, the crystals glowed, and the flames danced, licking the air around them as the power flowed through. This was not his biggest attempt. Just a test run for his next step.

"Did you notice Mr. Moon didn't open today?" a customer commented to Tara and Gran in the afternoon.

"I did," said Gran. "But I also heard his wife has been ill too. He has a sign on the door saying he had a family emergency, so perhaps she's having a bad day."

"Poor dear," the customer said. "I hope she's well soon. I've had my eye on this diamond necklace and I nearly have my husband convinced to get it for me."

Gran handed the purchase to the customer and shook her head when she left, but said nothing further about it. She grabbed a notepad and began writing as she addressed Tara.

"I need you to run to the Apothecary," she said. "I'm running low on some supplies." She tore off the list and handed it to Tara.

"Sure Gran, I'll head out now." Tara said as she walked out the store.

"Hello, Tara," Shylah said when she walked in. "I have everything here ready for your Gran. She called earlier to make sure I had it all, so I just went and packed it all up."

"Great," said Tara. "Mind if I browse for a bit?"

"Go right ahead," said Shylah, beaming. "If you have any questions, feel free to ask."

"Definitely." The first thing Tara noticed was the smell of the room. A mixture of incense and herbs flooded her senses. She looked at some of the jars along the wall behind the counter. Vanilla, chamomile, lavender, cherry blossom, spearmint, ginger were the ones she could pick out in the air, but there were many more.

She scanned a few of the display cases with assorted crystals. She ran her hand down an amethyst cluster and rotated it to see how the light caught it.

"I believe that is your Gran's birthstone, yes?" Shylah asked.

Tara nodded. She moved to the books almost naturally, and it wasn't long before she found a shelf of the assorted notebooks. She picked one that had a picture of a girl stroking a dragon. She ran her fingers along the image. The scales of the dragon were raised slightly, and the color shifted in the light. She had to buy it.

"Excellent choice," Shylah said. "I set one aside for myself."

"Gran suggested I start keeping notes of everything I've been learning," Tara said as she pulled out her wallet.

"That's a smart idea," said Shylah. "I have quite a few notebooks filled from my studies. You're welcome to come by anytime and browse through them. I've been considering setting up a kind of supernatural study group, but I don't know who else would even be interested."

"I would for sure," said Tara. "And Marissa definitely would be."

"I'll think about it," said Shylah. "I'll let you get back." She handed Tara all of her packages. "Stop by anytime. Or, shoot me a text if you have questions on anything. Gran has my number."

"Thanks so much," said Tara. She grabbed her bag and walked out.

"Hey! Tara! Over here." Tara turned and smiled when she saw Henry waving at her.

She waved back. "Hey there."

"I see you're doing better," he said.

"A lot better, thanks," said Tara.

"I was about to get some pizza at Aldo's Pizza Palace," said Henry, gesturing down the road. "Would you like to join me? It's a little place with a buffet that is phenomenal."

"I'm always up for some all-you-can-eat carbs," said Tara, laughing. "Just going to send Gran a text to let her know I'll be running late."

They walked further up the street and chatted about anything and everything. He filled her in on all of the town goings on while she was shut inside as they got a table in the restaurant.

"Aunt Sally finally had a day off today," Henry said. "So, she and Katrin went shopping and to have a spa day."

"Well, it is very well deserved," said Tara. "I have all the respect for people in the medical field. I had pneumonia when I was a freshman. I felt like I was a pain and the worst thing I did was ask when I could go home."

They arrived at Aldo's and stood in line for a minute to pay and get a table. The place was simply decorated. There was a small arcade at one end. And it smelled amazing. All of the smells of pizza and pasta that made Tara's stomach roar.

As they ate, Tara started to feel strange again. Her vision blurred. She saw little dark spots in front of her and her head throbbed so much she felt nauseous.

She noticed a few other people looking ill around them and something just felt off. Like there was something in the air. A presence of some kind, but she couldn't pinpoint it. The air felt heavy and the feeling of being watched made the hair on her arms stand on end.

"We need to get out of here," she said, pulling out her wallet.

"Are you okay?" Henry asked.

"I don't feel right again," she said. She left a big tip on the table and half stumbled out, with Henry following. Strangely, when they left the pizza place and started walking away, the feeling went away as well. She knew she had to tell Gran as soon as she got back home.

"I'm starting to feel a little tired again," she told Henry. "Is your car nearby?"

"At the end of the block," said Henry. "Want me to drive you home?"

"If you don't mind. I left my bike at home," said Tara. "I think I did too much today. Gran even pointed out that I hadn't had a single moment to decompress since finals before the first time this happened. So, I think I need to go home and curl up with a book."

"Okay," said Henry. "We will definitely have to try this again. Maybe the third time will be the charm."

"I hope so," said Tara. "What are you doing on July 4th? Gran's having her big cookout."

"I'm going out of town next week with some of my buds. I'll be gone for a few days."

"Sounds fun," said Tara.

They reached his truck. As Tara climbed in, she noticed something she must have missed last time. There was a long tooth tied to a small cord hanging from his mirror.

"What's that?" she asked, pointing to the mirror.

"Oh, it's nothing," Henry said. "Something I found in the woods."

They drove back to Kavanagh House and Henry walked Tara to the door. "You didn't have to do that," said Tara.

"I know," said Henry. "But you seemed a bit unsteady, still."

Tara blushed. "I appreciate your help," she said. "Do you want to hang out for a bit longer? It's such a nice day. I'm not ready for it to end." He nodded and sat with her on the porch swing.

"You look like you're ready to fall over again," he observed. "Catch your breath so your grandma doesn't worry."

"She always worries," said Tara. "She's probably trying to peek out at us through the curtains. I had a nice time with you again."

"Can I..." His cheeks went pink as he gestured to put his arm around her. She smiled and slid closer, allowing him and curling his fingers in hers. They sat in the swing, listening to the birds and watching the sky change as sunset approached. "Maybe we can go to the beach," said Henry. "There's a state park not far from here. The lake there is pretty big. They have boat rentals and fishing. The beach is great, never too crowded if you know where to go."

"I'd like that," said Tara.

"And, I like you," said Henry.

Tara turned, green eyes meeting gray, so close. "Henry..."

He placed his hand against her face. The warmth radiating against her. His fingers were rough. She shivered as he brushed a stray hair strand from her face. They held hands. She held her breath. And their lips met.

CHAPTER 10

Tara spent the next several minutes in a happy daze. Her cheeks felt hot and were probably the same shade as her hair. She felt lightheaded but not in the same way as in the restaurant. This was a good feeling. Butterflies fluttered in her stomach and she couldn't stop smiling.

When the kiss had ended, she smiled and Henry said goodnight. She watched him leave and just sat on the swing for a while, taking in the evening and replaying everything in her mind. A second date and a first kiss! She ran her tongue over her lips. She could kind of still taste it. The warmth of his lips on hers, soft and sweet. She tasted cherry lip balm and the subtle linger of spice from his dinner. She could smell his cologne hanging in the air, musky and a hint of something that reminded her of the burning wood at a bonfire. She recalled as his eyes darkened from light gray to near black like storm clouds. Was that... desire in his eyes?

Ha! Get real, she thought. She laughed out loud and stretched out across the swing, staring at the ceiling of the patio. Who would possibly want her? It wasn't like she was all that special. She didn't think she was pretty like Ruby Moon or Marissa. Or smart and witty like Gran. She was tall, curvy, and awkward. She was ordinary, aside from the whole being a witch thing. Even that, she was clueless about a lot of the magic still.

The creak of the front door opening and shutting jolted her back from her thoughts. Gran came out with a tray of tea and cookies. "Figured you could use a pick-me-up," she said as she poured the tea.

Tara thanked her and took a cookie. They were still warm from the oven. She sat back on the swing and closed her eyes as chocolate melted in her mouth.

"So, you had a pretty good night, all things considered," Gran said. At Tara's questioning look, Gran added, "I saw that he kissed you. Had to make sure he was being a gentleman."

"I just... he..." Tara beamed and continued to sit in silence. She ran a finger against her lip letting the kiss wash over her again.

Gran chuckled. "A first kiss is its own special kind of magic," she commented. "I remember mine with your grandpa. My granny, Lora, still lived with us. I thought she was going to turn him into a toad when she caught us. But, she just shrugged, said, "You better be good to her," and went about her day."

Tara laughed. "She sounds fun."

"She was the best," Gran said. She had a sad, wistful expression on her face as she spoke. "Helped out a lot after my father passed. With 6 mouths to feed and all four of us girls coming into their powers. My poor brothers. No wonder they couldn't wait to leave." They sat in silence some more, sipping tea and eating the cookies. "Seems like you might like this boy, if you let him kiss you."

Tara nodded. "I do. I don't know what'll happen, but I'm trying not to think about it and just enjoy my time being with him."

"What could happen?" Gran asked.

"He made a comment about how he thought the witchy stuff his aunt was interested in was weird. What if he finds out I'm a witch and... all the good things change?" Tara tucked her legs close. "I've learned so much in a short time and I haven't made a decision about giving it up. But, if I do, I may regret it."

"You can't decide that after 2 dates," said Gran. "Keep learning, see where that leads you. Like you said, enjoy your time and see where it goes. You're so young. You should date and have fun and enjoy your life. Settling down should be the furthest thing from your mind."

"Woah, woah, I never said anything about settling down yet," said Tara. She waved her hands and shook her head. "I'm just worried about not flunking out of college. I just have this thing where my brain likes to make up worst-case scenarios for no reason. It's been a lifelong struggle, especially when I'm tired."

"That's just anxiety, dear," Gran said with a chuckle. "I get it, too."

They went inside and Tara helped herself to a bowl of ice cream while Gran sorted through the bags of items Tara picked up for her.

"Something strange did happen today," said Tara. She explained the weird feeling she had at the Pizza Palace. "Weirdest part was, when we finally left, it started to go away."

Gran went pale. "Tell me exactly what you felt."

"I had spotty vision. I was queasy, and my head hurt," Tara said. "And I was dizzy when I stood up. If it was just my stomach, I would have said it was from too much pizza, but I don't think we were there more than an hour."

"Your mother had the same symptoms," Gran said. Her tone was serious.

Now it was Tara's turn to go pale. "Oh, God!" she whispered.

Gran took her hands. "We are going to figure this out. Marissa had some theories, so we should see what is in my books."

Tara scrambled for her phone and sent a text message to Marissa. "We need your help. More weird stuff happened in town. Get here ASAP."

CHAPTER 11

THE NEXT DAY, AFTER A LONG NIGHT OF RESEARCH, Marissa brought in the morning paper when she arrived at the shop with everyone's coffee. "There were more people admitted to the hospital with that weird illness," she said, pointing to the front page. "There are some who want to cancel Summer Fest next weekend in case it's a serious virus, but the Mayor says it's no big deal and everything will continue as normal."

"That's because he doesn't want to scare away tourists and their money," Gran commented as she counted the cash in the register.

Tara scanned the article. "Everyone who was admitted last night was at the Pizza Palace," she observed. "So, maybe this is what Henry and I felt and why it went away when we left."

"It's gotta be a spell," said Marissa.

"I have that feeling, too," said Tara. "And it's ramping up."

"Sounds like I need to make another call to Shylah," said Gran. "I have an idea for an investigation type spell that we can do but I need a few more items to make it work right."

"I can run over there for you," said Tara.

At about 8:00 that evening, Tara headed to the Apothecary. Shylah had everything Gran requested ready to go, so she was in and out quick. She put everything in a backpack, so it was easier to carry. And just in time to get a call from her mom. Fortunately, it was a normal voice call and not a video.

"Tara, I'm serious. I want you to come home."

"Hi Mom, thanks for calling," Tara said, not hiding the irritation in her tone. "I'm good. Thanks for asking."

"Tara Elizabeth, this is serious!" her mother snapped.

"What did you hear now?"

"The news picked up on some more weird stuff going on in that town and it's not safe."

"Who was their source?" Tara asked. "If it was anything by someone named Allan, it's bull. That's the Conspiracy Guy I warned you about."

"Maybe," said Mom. "I didn't pay attention. They showed a video about this restaurant and all these people getting sick and needing to go to the hospital."

"They probably had food poisoning," said Tara. "My friend Marissa said he exaggerates on purpose for the views. He's intentionally playing anyone gullible enough to fall for his stories. He's done it for years. And, if it's so dangerous here, why do you only want me to come home? What about Gran?

Or my friends? Or, you're just looking for a way to get me to give in still."

"I'm not going to keep having this darn argument with you," Mom said.

"Then please stop bringing it up!" Tara exclaimed. "Before I left, remember what you told me? You said you were proud of me. You said you wanted me to be happy. You said you didn't like it but you supported my wanting to come here. How about you try acting like it?"

"But…" her voice broke off.

"I have to go, Mom," Tara cut in. "I'm out running errands for Gran again and want to get back before it's dark."

Without waiting for her mother to reply, she tapped the screen to end the call. It was only then that she realized where she was. Lost. She was so absorbed in her conversation that she didn't pay attention to where she was going. She was in an alley somewhere.

"Oh, great," Tara said to herself. "Just what I need. First, I thought I landed in Charmed. Now, I'm in a slasher film cliche?"

She heard voices in the alley as she walked. She figured she could find a club or a restaurant and maybe someone would be nice enough to give her directions back to Gran's. The place reeked of rotting food from the trash bins of the nearby bars, and she didn't want to know what else was mixed in. A bottle shattered near her, causing her to jump, but it was only a cat knocking something off a dumpster.

A shadow moved out of the corner of her vision. She turned to see five guys, big, muscular, heavily drunk, and up to no good, step into the dim light from an open bar door. When they spotted her, they whispered to each other and started to laugh. Tara got a sick feeling in her stomach at what they might be thinking about.

"Lookie here, boys," said the biggest. He smacked a fist against his palm. He stood, broad shouldered and about 6'4". He was easily 400 pounds of muscle on top of beer belly, making him look like an extremely large football player or a small sumo wrestler. His speech was slurred, and he reeked of whiskey, among other things, confirming Tara's theory that he was drunk. "The lady looks lost." His cronies guffawed in agreement. "I think we should have some fun before we help her find her way home."

"Great," said Tara, knowing her increasing irritation would get her in trouble, but she was too frightened to care. "Harass a girl half your size. Yeah, you're a real manly man, aren't you?"

"Whachu tryin' say, ya fat bitch?" barked one of the guys. He staggered forward a few steps, trying to look intimidating. He puffed out his chest and cracked his knuckles. He looked small, compared to the apparent leader of the group, but still easily had 100 pounds on her.

"Oh, wow, like I've never been called that before!" Tara exclaimed. "I mean, aside from the fact that you need to learn how to speak in complete words and sentences? I don't want any trouble. I am just trying to go home."

"Hey, I seen you around," said the first. "You, that old lady's grandkid. That freaky Irish broad."

"She's Scottish," Tara grumbled. It was a common mistake that tended to irritate her grandmother, who was very proud of their heritage and the country of her birth. "And you need a lesson in manners as well as third grade grammar and geography." She hoped that attempting a brave face would make them back off. It wasn't working. They were either that drunk or that stupid not to get the hint. Probably both.

They surrounded her. Like a pack of wolves around their prey. A couple of them panted and drooled like the low-life dogs they were. She had nowhere to run. And she was not strong enough to fight them. Why hadn't she paid attention to where she was going? She should have told her mother she was busy and gotten off the phone. But, no. She was pulled into another debate about her life choices and look where it landed her. Her hands gripped the handle of her bags and she felt her nails dig into her palms.

"I'm warning you," she said, her last attempt at bravado failing miserably as her voice trembled. "Just back off and let me go home."

"We'll let you go," said the one who had called her a bitch. "When we've had our fun."

He lunged forward with a roar. For being so huge, he was fast. He grabbed her from behind as she turned to run and held her arms tight against her back. She cried out as he groped her chest and planted a slobbering kiss on her cheek. She wanted to gag at the stench of him. A sickening mixture of body odor from not showering in Lord knew how long, cheap cigars, weed smoke, and whiskey on his breath. The leader of the group stepped forward, and Tara did not like the look in his eyes.

Oh my God, she thought, fighting to keep the tears from filling her eyes. *Someone, please, help me!*

"Hey!"

The group turned and Tara cried out when she saw who had shouted. "Henry, get out of here!"

Henry stepped more into the lamp light. His face was partly shadowed, and it almost seemed like his gray eyes glowed. He glared at the group, fists clenched, body tense, ready to spring. "Leave her alone," he growled.

"Want to have some fun with us, McKenna?" said the creep holding Tara. He grabbed her hair and pulled her head back. Tara strained against him. "She's pretty. For a chunker." He licked her neck from her shoulders to her cheek and laughed when she whimpered in disgust. Her stomach recoiled, and she was almost thankful she didn't have anything to eat since lunch.

"I said leave her alone," Henry repeated, the growl in his tone intensified to a snarl and scared Tara even more. Was that even possible? She had never seen him angry before.

One of the group, a big, bald guy this time, charged him and moved to throw a wild punch but took a blow in the stomach as a reward. Tara thought she heard a rib crack as the boy fell to the ground in pain, clutching his side and howling.

Now, 3 of the 4 remaining thugs rounded on Henry. Tara struggled, but that only made her captor hold her tighter. He laughed every time she tried to move. He pulled her close and she could feel in more ways than one that he was enjoying it. She closed her eyes when the punching started. Partly because she couldn't stand the sight of Henry getting pummeled. Partly to keep herself from gagging from the stench of the guy who continued to grab and grope. If she made it, she was going to go home and take a scalding shower to try to get the grime off her.

After a few minutes, Tara heard the sound of an unconscious body hit the ground. Punches and kicks continued, though.

Oh, no! Are they still beating him? Tara thought, horrified.

"Where the hell did you come from?" she heard Henry ask.

Tara opened her eyes. One creep was on the ground, nose bloody. The one with the possible broken rib was cowering by the dumpster. The other two were now squaring off with Henry and "Mr. Moon?" Tara cried.

"Hi, Tara," Mr. Moon shouted as he circled his opponent. He dodged a clumsy blow with the speed and grace of a panther. Tara thought he must have had training in whatever he wanted. He probably could afford to hire Chuck Norris.

Henry, too, was an impressive fighter. But, where Mr. Moon's style was based on skill and agility, Henry was raw emotion, aggression, and pure strength. Still, he was holding his own. Strangely, Tara found it quite attractive. Every time he started to come closer to fight the guy holding her, one of the others would appear and block his progress.

Tara was on her own, for now anyway. She had to figure out how to break free of the coward, using her as a human shield to keep out of the brawl. If she could get out of the alley and call the police while Henry and Mr. Moon had these guys occupied, they would be taken off and not be able to bother anyone for a very long time, if she had her way. But she had to get to that point first. Without drawing attention to herself would be ideal, but that didn't look like an available option.

It was like a lightbulb went off in her head. She did have a way out. How could she forget this already? Maybe it was the fear and adrenaline clouding her thoughts. But she was, after all, a witch. She knew exactly what to do.

Concentrating with all her might, or as much as she could while being held captive and unwillingly getting glimpses in her mind of what would happen to her if she couldn't get away, she envisioned a flame on the guy's shoe just like she had practiced with Marissa and Gran. She could see the glow of it out of the corner of her eye and feel the heat as the flame burst to life.

It took a minute for the genius to realize his foot was on fire. The flames had licked away his shoe and were working through his sock. The unmistakable scent of burning leather, rubber, and flesh filled her nostrils, mixed with the smell he already had. It made her head spin, and she fought off nausea with her remaining strength. The smell was followed by the guy howling in pain and releasing her.

She stumbled before she flew into Henry's arms as the thugs ran off. Sirens sounded at the end of the alley and shouts of "Get on the ground!" could be heard.

Tara and Henry stared at Mr. Moon, who laughed and held up his phone. "I heard the commotion and told the police to be waiting," he said with a grin.

They took turns giving statements to the police about what happened. A thousand questions ran through Tara's head, but she was able to voice one. She whirled on Henry. "Did you know those guys?"

He looked down quickly. "Yes, unfortunately," he said quietly. Then he met her eyes. "I went to school with them. They're real f-ing jerks."

"Really?" said Mr. Moon sarcastically as he tucked his phone back in his pocket. "I thought your friends were quite charming."

"We're not friends," Henry barked. "I knew them from high school. That's all." He turned back to Tara. "And I am so sorry they went after you like that. Are you okay? Did... did they do anything?" He asked with a shudder running through his voice. "What were you doing here, anyway?"

"I got lost," said Tara. "What were you doing here?"

"On my way to a band gig." He pointed to the guitar case propped along the wall. And his eyes went wide as he looked at his watch. "Shit! I'm late! I gotta go. Do you want to come watch? And I'll take you home after?"

Tara shook her head. "Raincheck," she said. "I think I've had a bit too much excitement for one evening. I'm going home to get some tea and sleep."

"I can cancel, if you want," Henry suggested. "The guys can play without me. It'll just sound a little off."

Tara shook her head again. "No, it's okay. I can call Gran."

"Are you sure?" he asked.

Tara gave him a little nudge. "Go. Your friends are depending on you and adoring fans await."

"If you insist. Just let me know when you get home, okay? I'll see you later." Henry gave her a kiss on the cheek and ran down the alley into one of the bars. Shouts and cheers were followed by music.

Tara's head pounded in beat with the drums as she reached for her phone.

"I can give you a ride home," Mr. Moon said. "We're just going to have some explaining for your grandma."

"Yeah," said Tara. "I think she'll be okay once she hears the story."

"What's in the bag?" Mr. Moon asked, glancing out the corner of his eye as they drove.

"Some stuff from the Apothecary," Tara said. "Gran... uh... makes teas and stuff with herbs. But sometimes she needs special ingredients that she can only get there." She quickly examined the items in the bag and sighed in relief as everything was still, miraculously, intact.

"Hmm," was all Mr. Moon responded. Tara wasn't paying much attention.

They pulled into the driveway at Kavanagh House and Gran ran out. "I just heard on my scanner what happened. Oh, you poor dear!" She pulled Tara into a hug. "Are you okay? What happened?" She saw Mr. Moon getting out of the car and hugged him as well. "Oh, thank you. Once again, Mr. Moon, you have my gratitude. Will you come in for some cookies?"

"No, Ms. Kavanagh, but thank you," he said. "I need to get home and check on my wife."

"Of course, of course," she said. "At least let me pack some up for you."

"She won't let you go unless she does that," Tara said quietly. "Also, her cookies are amazing, so…"

"Alright," Mr. Moon finally relented.

Gran led them through the house to the kitchen. Mr. Moon stepped out onto the porch with Tara, admiring the scenery of the yard. "Quite a garden," he commented.

"Gran's pride," said Tara. "She's worked on it for a long time. By contrast, I'm trying to cure my black thumb. I either forget to water or overdo it, and all my plants die."

Mr. Moon chuckled. "Same. My wife, Ruby, is brilliant with plants. When we get a house, I am going to build a greenhouse in the yard."

At that moment, Gran returned with a large plastic container of assorted cookies. Mr. Moon's eyes went wide. "You didn't have to…"

"Yes, I did. Now, go see your wife and thank you again, Mr. Moon."

"Call me Ethan, please," he said. "We're business neighbors. But no need to be so formal."

"Alright then," said Gran. "Thank you, Ethan." He took the tray, waved, and walked around to the front of the house, back to his car.

When he was gone, Gran turned her attention to Tara. "Now, you need to tell me everything. And I DO mean everything."

"We need to keep an eye on all three of them, I think," Darien told Lilia. "The redhead has power. I knew it given her family but I witnessed it tonight. It's still largely raw, emotional, and untapped, but it is there. And the other two are powerful. The old Scottish lady has experience on her side, along with that honed power. Haven't seen much from the other girl yet but it's a matter of time, I'm sure."

"Who do you think is the bigger threat?" she asked.

"None of them individually," he said. "Especially the redhead. All three joining forces could be what will unravel everything."

"We'll be on our guard, then," she said. "Find ways to... inconvenience them when the next phase of your plan takes place."

He chuckled. "I love when you're scheming," he said. He stepped closer to the mirror. "It's so... seductive."

She giggled and held her hand up, motioning running a finger down his cheek. "I can't wait to cause all sorts of trouble when I'm out of here."

"You will, my dearest," he said. "Soon."

CHAPTER 12

MARISSA SAT IN THE BASEMENT ANNEX AT KAVANAGH House surrounded by books. She had brought one of the beanbag chairs from the office with her. The stools near the old table were so rickety and old she always waited for them to crumble when someone sat down. The room had plenty of electric light, but she also lit a white candle to set the mood and help her focus.

She tried to come up with some way they could detect what was going on with these people ending up in the hospital. Ms. Kavanagh and Tara were working that morning and she had the day off. Using her spare key, and informing Ms. K of what she wanted to do, of course, Marissa let herself in when she finished tending to things at home, brewed some strong coffee, and fully dove into research mode.

There was just one problem. She didn't know where to even start. Only thing they knew was people seemed to just get exhausted and pass out and there was some sort of force behind it if you were sensitive enough to pick it up. Once you were away from that force, it seemed to get better. She decided to grab a notebook and write out her thoughts to see if that led somewhere she could try.

"Alright," she wrote, just letting her pen move as the stream of thoughts came to her mind. "According to Tara, the symptoms are basically being exhausted. May start as a slight disruption in concentration and focus. Zoning out, that kind of thing. Then it progresses to light-headedness and feeling like you're going to pass out. Last time it happened, she got away from it and the feeling went away. That's when she thought she sensed something. But, for the first time, even when she left, she still ended up passing out. So, what was different? If this was a spell, what kind of spell?"

She stopped writing for a minute, flexed her fingers as she tried to think of what to write next, recalling what she, Tara, and Gran had discussed or heard from people in town.

"Clearly," she wrote, "it drains people's energy, but for what purpose? Another question to figure out. And it could have been targeted that first time. Like at Mr. Moon's opener. One or two people, but everyone around them was fine. Then, a more broad application. But what are the triggers for the target? Is it something about those people or is it random? Someone could have found out about Tara being from a line of witches. But how does that explain Lydia being a target? She's not a threat to anyone. She's just a sweet lady who's probably never even swatted a fly. And she's pregnant. Gotta be a special kind of sick to target a poor pregnant lady."

Marissa set her pen down and did a few stretches. She had almost filled a page with her thoughts. And it just created more unanswered questions.

She took another sip of her coffee and decided the best way to find answers was to be more proactive. She grabbed her phone and sent a text to Tara and Ms. Kavanagh. "Hey, I think we should do a general 'Something is up.' I can prep everything for when you get back. Looks like we have everything here. I might grab some things from my house that I just prefer using."

"Do what you need to do, love," was Ms. Kavanagh's reply immediately followed by a thumbs up from Tara. "We'll try to get out of here as soon as possible."

Marissa ran back upstairs, hopped on her bike, and raced home to grab what she needed. When she was satisfied, she returned to Kavanagh House to prepare the spell.

Tara and Gran returned later that evening, and everything was ready in the basement. All of the furniture was pushed along the walls to make space except for a table in the center of the room. Several white taper candles in little holders were arranged in a circle around that. Marissa set a stick of vanilla and coconut incense in a holder and placed it on the table.

"So, what's going on?" asked Tara.

"It's a basic ritual," Marissa explained. "It's pretty much like asking the forces that be, whatever you want to call them, to help us find out what's going on. We light candles, burn some incense, and try to get into a state to see what we can discover beyond what's clear to our eyes. Lifting the veil essentially." She passed over her notebook. "I did some brainstorming and just had more questions piling up, so I knew the books wouldn't be much help. When in doubt, we try a spell."

Gran skimmed the notes Marissa had made. "These are very good questions, though. We'll talk about what you came up with after we try the spell. Keep this notebook handy. It'll help organize all our information."

Marissa stuck the pen inside the notebook and put it on one of the shelves along the wall. She handed Tara and Gran each a lighter. "We light the candles," she explained, mostly for Tara. "I'll light the incense. I like this blend because it smells amazing and coconut is good for protection and purification." She gestured to the other items. "There's also a bowl of water and soil. All of this combined represents the four elements– earth, air, fire and water." She glanced at Gran. "I know, we do things a bit differently."

Gran just waved a hand. "My dear, you're leading this. I'm just going along for the ride."

Marissa nodded and dimmed the lights, so the candles seemed to glow even brighter. They stood in the space she had cleared in the center of the room. "For some added protection, we'll create a circle. Just imagine a ring of light surrounding us."

Tara closed her eyes and tried to do what she was told. She focused on Marissa's words as she had in their other lessons, and that helped direct her concentration. She visualized a ring of light around them. And, more than seeing, she felt it. Soothing and warm, like having a guardian watching them work. She listened as Marissa spoke the words of the spell, and she and Gran repeated it two more times with her.

"Unseen, unknown, but causing harm

A threat that causes pain and alarm.

Earth, Air, Fire, water

All the elements, hear as we ask

Lift the veil, pull it back

Show us what we seek and ask

That this threat to be unmasked."

Each time, Tara felt further and further away from where they were. They saw a clearing in the woods. The details had a hazed look about them, like a fog or a dream sequence on a television show. Then, slowly, things began to focus. The details on the trees, the moon in the sky approaching full with countless stars visible on the clear summer night. Then, other details that did not seem like they belong tripped the senses. The smell of strong incense and candle smoke, the feeling of strong, dark power.

Tara felt Gran tense and her anxiety radiated from her. Marissa tried to move a bit further, but something blocked them. It was strong. They heard laughter and then whoosh! The feeling of something grabbing her around the belly and yanking hard. They spiraled back into reality, back in the basement causing them all to collapse in a heap.

"What..." Tara panted. "What in the name of heaven and hell was that?"

"I don't know," Marissa managed. She rolled over onto her knees and grabbed a small garbage can, but only was able to dry heave. Tara, shaking and tears streaming down her cheeks, handed her a paper towel to wipe the blood coming from her nose. "I've never touched anything like that before."

The girls turned to Gran. She was pale and shaking, Tara would even say frightened. She crawled over and pulled her grandmother into a hug. "Gran! Are you okay?"

Gran just nodded. They sat in silence for a few minutes, with the sound of Marissa's continued heaves as the only sound in the room. When everyone was calm and quiet, Gran spoke. "Whoever is doing this is incredibly powerful. And they picked up on what we were trying to do. The protection we laid out wasn't enough."

"I could tell," said Marissa, as she fought the sickness in her stomach. "Did you detect that emotion? It was dark, violent."

"Angry," said Tara. "All of that. Just rage and frustration that has been building for a while. Like a volcano ready to blow."

"No," said Gran. "More like… righteousness. The sense of he knows he's hurting people while doing this, but he doesn't care. It was the same feeling when we realized what was happening to your mother. But, this–this time something felt different… it was a need, almost a hunger… this time I sensed desperation. Like you said, Tara. This has been building."

"Even I picked up on that," said Tara. "Desperation, maybe fear?"

"I'm so tempted to quote Star Wars right now," said Marissa with a smirk. "You know what Yoda says about fear."

Tara managed a giggle. "Glad I wasn't the only one."

"The area seemed familiar, too," Marissa said. "It's gotta be close to town. Somewhere in the park?"

"Unless he had a cloaking spell, someone would have walked into where this is," said Gran. "Could be in the woods just outside of town. But it's close. It would have to be if we stumbled on it."

"I think we should try again," said Marissa. "See if we can maybe get anything more."

"Not today," said Gran. "I can't." She held out her hands, and both girls helped her to her feet. She immediately grabbed the nearest bench to sit before she collapsed again. "That was a full knockout. You got a nosebleed. Tara's still recovering somewhat and this was her first time experiencing that much power. I haven't done anything like that in years. We need to recover for a while, take time to consider what we were able to learn." She pointed to the notebook Marissa had set on the shelf.

"Maybe I can do a locator spell–if we locate the place of the spell, it'll give us some more clues on who it is behind this and visit the spot in person," said Marissa. "Do some snooping."

"That is stupidly dangerous!" Gran blurted. Marissa gaped at her forceful tone. "Look, I know you want to figure this out. So do I. We've confirmed this is supernatural, and that's a start. But, we don't know how powerful this person or creature or whatever actually is. What if this was just a percentage of capable power? It knocked all three of us for a loop. We need time and preparation to know how to continue further."

Marissa nodded, but still looked irritated. They headed back upstairs. Gran put on some of her healing tea while Marissa put a collection of herbs, pepper, bay leaf, rosemary, and lavender in a little pouch for each of them. She handed one to Tara with some words written on a piece of paper. "Say this spell and put the herbs under your pillow tonight," she instructed. "It'll help keep out mental intruders and prevent nightmares."

"Thanks," said Tara. She tucked it in her pocket.

Marissa turned to Gran. "I think I'm gonna crash here tonight if you don't mind," she said. "I am a little unsteady to bike home and I am actually a little shaken up."

"You know you're always welcome here, love," Gran said.

"You can sleep in my room if you want," Tara said. "I don't really want to be alone either."

That night, as the girls got ready for bed, Tara kept thinking about the spell they tried. Replaying the images that flashed in her head–then the shock of being pulled back.

"Did I..." she paused, trying to pick her words carefully. "Was I the reason we got caught? That the ritual stopped like it did?"

"No, why would you think that?" Marissa asked as she unfolded the cot Gran had brought up.

"Well, like Gran said, I'm new at all this," Tara said. She fiddled with a loose string on her pajamas. "I wasn't powerful enough to keep up the protection and keep us hidden."

Marissa sat on the bed and took Tara's hands in hers. "First of all," she said. "I take blame for some of it. Thinking we could manage with a simple circle was a huge underestimation on my part. Second, we went in blind and we got our asses handed to us because of it. It's nobody's fault except the person who is doing whatever this is to make people sick. You've got power. It just needs to be honed in a bit and strengthened. But, if you decide to keep learning and developing, you'll be amazing. It's in your blood. You can't teach that kind of magic. You're powerful. Just look at your Gran. She's been practicing her whole life and I bet there are plenty of things she still has to learn."

Tara thought for a moment. "It's like writing," she said. "You can't just slap words on a page, upload it, and expect the cash to flow. You have to edit and develop your craft."

"And, with each draft, it gets better, right?" said Marissa. "Same thing goes for magic and anything else. With each spell you do, the more you learn, the more you develop your power. So, it goes from raw and rough to more skilled and refined. And, you keep learning because there's always something new. Or some people specialize in a couple of things."

Tara felt better as she climbed into bed. She put the pouch of herbs under the pillow. "You still want to try again, though."

"Abso-freaking-lutely," said Marissa. She stood back up and unrolled her sleeping bag onto the cot. "Going to try to make a case for tomorrow. I want to find out what's going on and kick some magical hiney. But I also understand your Gran's point about being reckless."

They said the protection spell together and turned out the lights. Tara breathed in the smell of lavender, dried coconut, and anise in the pouch Marissa had given her, letting them soothe her mind. She drifted off to a pleasant, restful sleep.

~

First thing in the morning, the trio was back in the basement annex room to try the same ritual again. This time, they did a little more to try to prepare and protect themselves. More candles. More incense. Marissa lined the circle with black tourmaline crystals for even more protection.

They said the spell again and saw the area in the woods almost instantly. They moved through the area, trying to take in every detail. But, as they reached where they were the night before, they were pushed back twice as hard.

A cold chill ran down Tara's spine as they heard a voice in their heads.

"I rarely give second chances. I will not give you a third. Stay out of my way." The voice growled with each syllable.

Marissa and Tara both felt sick this time. Gran took several more minutes to recover. When she was able to stand, she grabbed every item she could that represented cleansing and protection.

"I am not risking anything getting in here," she explained. She handed the girls armfuls of items to help her place in every room of the house. Then recited a cleansing spell. "How about we go out for breakfast?" she suggested. "The house should be vacant, so the spell can take effect."

"Sounds like a plan," said Marissa.

"Yes, please," said Tara.

He dropped to the floor, fists clenched, fighting the urge to roar. He felt the sting of fingernails digging into flesh so hard that he drew blood. His heart raced, his face felt hot. He wanted to explode. Then he felt a cold sensation on his cheek. Goosebumps raised on his arms. He looked into her eyes and instantly melted. But some of his irritation remained.

The force gathered from this latest attempt allowed her to emerge, briefly, from the mirror, but she was a ghost. She floated a few inches above the floor, almost transparent. It was a step, so he had to be thankful for that. He just hoped that it wouldn't have negative after effects for her.

"I should have ended them," he growled. He sat back on the floor and she sat curled up into him, still hovering slightly. She leaned her head on his shoulder. The intent of the gesture made him smile, even if he couldn't feel anything in her current state.

"Then who will I have to play with when I'm all better?" she said, her tone sad and pouting, but the wicked twinkle shined in her eyes. "They won't figure it out. And if they do, it'll be too late to do anything."

CHAPTER 13

Tara and Marissa took Gran's advice about not repeating the spell again, but that didn't mean they stopped trying to figure things out. During every moment of downtime at work, Tara had a pen and her journal in hand, trying to recall everything from the events of the spell, and both times she had whatever that penetrating feeling of weakness was. Over lunch, the girls sat in Gran's office. Marissa brought one of her larger sketchbooks and drew what she believed the clearing area looked like, and Gran and Tara filled in details as she worked.

"Everything focused in the center of that clearing," said Gran. Marissa drew a circle and a question mark. "Were you able to see anything about that area?"

"I smelled smoke, so there are either candles or a fire," Tara commented. "I think it was candles. It's different from my other dream."

"The lighting would have been different, too," said Marissa. "And it was nearly dark when we saw the area. If there was a fire burning, we'd know." She sketched a bit more, just letting her fingers move with the pencil, almost on autopilot. She held up the image for a minute. A rough sketch of a clearing in the middle of some woods. There were candles and the center part was shaded to signify that they weren't sure exactly what was there. "I think I know where this is. There's a spot just at the edge of the park, not far from the square. I used to walk there sometimes. It's a kind of spooky area."

"That helps," said Gran. "But I still wouldn't go there. If the source of this can sense us using a spell, they would definitely know if you were just strolling in."

"We could try a glamour," said Marissa. "Or set up some kind of distraction to lure them out?"

Gran shook her head. "I have a feeling they would see through that, too," she said. "We will consider and plan a bit more. We have plenty to do in the meantime with the holiday this weekend."

The lead up to July 4th weekend, and Coolersville Summer Fest, flew by so time for research became minimal at best, usually resulting in Tara falling asleep while reading. While there were some calls to postpone Summer Fest due to the people who were sick, the Mayor and city council doubled down and insisted there was nothing wrong, welcoming all tourists.

On the actual holiday, almost all the shops closed in observance, except the grocery store and the drugstore. Most of the restaurants remained open as well to take advantage of people gathering in and around town. It looked like the whole town was suddenly draped in flags and red, white, and blue streamers.

Crowds lined Main Street for the big parade that morning. Tara sat with Marissa and Gran in lawn chairs in front of the shop. They even managed a pass for Marissa's sweet grandma, Lorraine, for a few hours.

Marissa couldn't help smiling as her Nana pointed and laughed at the floats the various organizations around town had put together. She clapped and sang along with every band and every vehicle that passed them, playing a patriotic tune.

Several people stopped to say hi and ask how she was coming along. Nana was happier than Marissa had seen her in several months. So, she made a point to try to make sure Nana had more regular outings over the summer. Once her semester started, it would be difficult to visit, let alone take her out for the day.

As they watched the Pride Dancers, the performers from Attitude, glide by on their giant rainbow float, they heard someone calling out to them. Two middle-aged women and a girl a bit older than Tara and Marissa practically ran over to them. One, a tall, heavy set woman with short, curly brown hair and glasses, hugged Marissa. The other woman was also tall, but slender. She had long, dark brown hair streaked with gray that fell almost to her butt. The girl had dark hair as well. She was slightly shorter.

"Hello!" said the short haired woman when she saw Tara. "I'm Nancy McKenna, Henry's mom. I'm so happy to finally meet you!"

Tara shook her hand and was immediately pulled into a hug.

"Nan, you're embarrassing the poor girl," said the other woman. "She's as red as her hair."

"Oh, hush," Nancy said. But she pulled back. "This is my sister, Sally, and my niece, Katrin."

"Hi," Tara said softly. "Not to be rude, but how did you know who I was?"

"Henry described you to us," said Katrin. "We know Marissa since they went to school together and everyone knows your grandma. So, we put 2 and 2 together."

"I'm sorry my son couldn't be here," Nancy continued. "He insists on going on those wretched boys trips with his friends. I mean, I suppose it's good, but he misses so much of our family time."

"Would you like to join us, Mrs. McKenna?" Gran offered. "I have some extra chairs in the car."

"Oh, thank you so much!" Nancy said. "We did bring our own. We'll get them and be right back."

They chatted with Henry's family throughout the parade. Tara already knew that Aunt Sally worked as an Emergency Room nurse at the hospital. Katrin was in her second year of nursing school. She wanted to work in the NICU. Mrs. McKenna was a librarian at the elementary school.

Still being unfamiliar, Tara stayed relatively quiet and tried to keep her nerves down. They seemed like perfectly nice people. It was the added detail of being the family of the boy she liked that added the unsubstantiated anxiety.

"What are you studying at the college?" Mrs. McKenna asked.

Tara took a deep breath. "I'm not sure yet," she said. "I named journalism, but I don't really know if that's what I'm sticking to."

"You don't have things figured out yet?" Mrs. Tillman called, followed by laughter. Tara turned to see Mrs. Tillman glaring at them. Her horrible twins made faces and rude gestures behind her back along with another girl, a tall skinny blond who looked the same age as Tara and Marissa.

"Why don't you mind your business?" Katrin snapped.

"I just don't understand how you can be accepted to a school and not know what you're doing," Mrs. Tillman said. "I knew what I wanted when I was twelve. And I worked every day until I got what I want."

"Back off, Anya," said Sally. "You don't know anything about her or her life. Not everyone has to know what they want out of life at 18. I certainly didn't. I'm 58 and I still don't know sometimes. But whatever Tara decides, it will be wonderful."

"Certainly better than being over-botoxed arm candy for a sleazebag politician," Katrin said, and everyone laughed.

"Well, I never!" Mrs. Tillman turned and stormed off, muttering about how rude people can be.

After the parade, Marissa rode with Gran to take Nana back to the nursing home where she was staying as she recovered from a severe stroke. She still wasn't strong enough to come home. And Marissa wanted to make sure she was cared for once school started. Home care was an option, but it was limited. At least Marissa could feel better with the 24 hour care at Sunnyside.

She helped Nana into bed and they returned to Kavanagh House for the annual cook-out. As she talked and ate and played with Rose's children, Marissa's thoughts kept wandering to the clearing. She kept seeing glimpses of it in her mind. The need to investigate, to see for herself seemed to call to her. She knew it was dangerous. What had Gran called it? Stupidly dangerous. But, everyone was busy with festivities. Maybe this person was, too.

Marissa had her opportunity that night. They returned to town for the big fireworks show. Phone at the ready, she slipped away from her friends and headed in the general direction of the clearing.

Unaware, Gran and Tara watched the show. The college radio station had set up a booth, and the fireworks were coordinated to go off to a series of songs. People were dancing and laughing and every worry slipped away.

…Until someone screamed.

Tara's heart stopped. The sound pierced the night. The cheers of the spectators stopped. Tara and Gran heard Rose shrieking as Amelia lay limp in her arms. More screams and cries as more people suddenly dropped to the ground. Tara jumped when she felt a hand grab her, but it was only Gran.

"Do you feel that?" she asked quietly.

Tara forced herself to focus. The same feeling she had the last time she and Henry had gone out was back in full force. "We need to get out of here."

"Where's Marissa?" Gran pointed out. They looked around and called out, but the sudden stampede of people brought that to a swift end.

"Look out!" Tara tried to pull Gran along with her, but it was just too much and they lost each other in the crowd. People running, some carrying family members, some struggling to walk, some both as the power of whatever this was overwhelmed them and they became among those now unconscious all over the square. Tara found Gran on the ground, holding her knee.

"I can't…" she began.

"My car isn't far, and you're bleeding," Tara said. "We'll get you to the hospital."

"Marissa…"

"I'll come back and try to find her."

She helped Gran stand, and they slowly moved to the car. Gran directed her to the hospital, just off the college campus. They pulled into the Emergency Room and spotted Henry's aunt, Sally. Sally made sure Gran was admitted as she also had a nasty abrasion on her head.

"What about the people coming in?" the receptionist asked. "Phones are ringing off the hook."

"Head injury!" was all Sally said. "Make it happen. We'll manage with the rest."

She grabbed a wheelchair and moved Gran to a room, Tara close on her heels. "I thought you were here about Marissa," she told Tara.

"What about Marissa?"

"She was brought in about 10 minutes ago," Sally explained. "Someone found her near the woods. Her phone was busted up, and she looked like she'd been in a fight. She also has a bump on the head and maybe this exhaustion thing because she hasn't come to yet. She's breathing, though."

As she spoke, Gran's phone buzzed in her purse. Tara grabbed it and saw a flood of messages, photo and video files and one text message that said, "I found it."

Sally helped Gran settle in and when they were alone, Tara showed her the phone. "I told her not to!" Gran exclaimed.

"Look who we're talking about," said Tara. "Looks like she got caught," she observed as she scrolled. "Some of these files aren't coming through. That explains her phone getting busted. I might be able to get it going if I can hook it up to my computer."

"Check the file saver program on mine," said Gran. "All of her photos are automatically backed up so we can pick out the prints she sells in the shop. I'll give you the password."

"Alright," said Tara. "But I want to make sure you're okay first and then I'll get to work."

CHAPTER 14

Just after midnight, Tara talked quietly with her dad on the phone in Gran's hospital room. Marissa was still asleep and bruised, but otherwise okay. Gran was undergoing some more tests and had her knee x-rayed. Doctors determined her knee was sprained. They were waiting for the results of her head scan.

To get her mind off things, she had gone home to try to recover the photos. She tried not to focus on the details of them until she returned to Gran. She just wanted to make sure it worked. When it finally did, she sent them to her own phone along with printing them. She knew she should stay home and sleep, but she also knew she'd just be worrying until Gran's results came back. So, she put everything in her bag and returned to the hospital.

She sat down, pulled out the envelope, and was just about to go through everything with Gran as they waited for tests. That was when her father had called.

"Yes, she's doing okay," Tara said. "I mean, as okay as you can be stuck in a hospital bed... No, you don't need to come down here... Why? Because Mom will have a panic attack and expect you to come home with me in tow. Just tell her what I told you. Someone got stupid with a popgun and people panicked."

As she ended the call, Henry walked in. Gran slipped the envelope back in Tara's purse so there weren't any questions. "I came as soon as I could," he said as she flew into his arms. He sent Gran a shy smile. "Hi, Ms. Kavanagh. How are you feeling?"

"I've been better," she said, showing the lump of compression wrappings on her knee and the bandage around her head. "But I'll live a bit longer."

"How did you know?" Tara asked. "And how did you get back here?"

"I got a call from a friend and then Aunt Sally texted me, letting me know what happened with Gran," he said. "Said you might need someone."

"You didn't have to cut your trip short for me," said Tara.

"We would have been home tomorrow, or later today given the time," Henry explained, glancing at his watch. "Besides, my mom was having a total breakdown, so yes, I did have to come home. She doesn't handle negative things very well. But, before I go home, I can sit with you a while. Maybe we can go to the cafeteria to get some coffee?"

"Yes, please," Tara said. "I have to drive home in a bit."

"You are not!" exclaimed Gran.

"It's not that far," Tara argued. "I went home earlier to... uh... get those things you needed."

"No, you're too tired," said Gran. "It's dangerous."

"I can give you a ride," said Henry. "I'm hopped up on energy drinks and my sleep schedule is off, so I'll be up for a while yet."

"No, thank you, though," said Tara. "I can get some more coffee and be okay. Gran has to go over how to do her paperwork before I leave." She gestured to the envelope sticking out of her purse.

"Oh, right," said Gran. "That is important. Must have slipped my mind. Head injury and all." She tapped at her head.

Tara and Henry walked to the cafeteria. There was a small counter selling coffee and bakery items still open at the late hour, so they each got a large coffee, heavy on the cream, and a couple of stale donuts.

They sat at a table and ate their treat in silence for a minute. "Thanks," Tara said finally. "You didn't have to come. And, if your mom is freaking out, you should probably get going. I'm gonna leave as soon as this last test comes back."

"You sure you're going to be okay driving?" Henry asked. "It's not that much to give you a ride, really. I'm used to my mom freaking out."

"Yeah, but if your aunt is working late, someone should be there with your mom," said Tara.

"What about you going home alone?"

"I'll be okay. I'll probably work on the papers for a while or write to clear my head," she said. "Also, Gran makes this really good tea that will help anyone sleep."

"Hmm, I'll have to get you to hook me up with some for my mom." Henry's phone buzzed. "That's my aunt," he said when he read the text. "The tests are back."

They grabbed their coffees and headed back to the room. A doctor was there with his clipboard. When they entered, he paused. "It's okay, Doctor," said Gran. "This is my granddaughter and her boyfriend. They can hear what you have to say."

Henry and Tara just turned bright red. "We're just friends," Tara muttered, staring at the floor.

"Alright then." The doctor cleared his throat. "The good news is no concussion."

"Woo!" Tara blurted out. She quickly turned even more red and went quiet. "Sorry."

"We would like to do another check on your knee, though," he went on. "You landed pretty hard. Want to make sure there's no bone chipping or anything like that. So we're going to keep you overnight for observation and you should be able to go home tomorrow after we do some more scans."

"Good," said Gran. "Thank you, Doctor."

The doctor walked out with Sally. And Tara turned to Henry. "You should get home before your mom sends out a real search party."

"Alright," he said. "Still send me a text when you get back home so I know you're okay."

"You, too," said Tara.

"Yes, Mom."

Tara poked him in the stomach, but then gave him a peck on the cheek. He turned red and walked out smiling. Tara grabbed the envelope from her bag and slid the door shut.

"Before we do this, I need a favor," Gran said. "Text Rose. I know it's late, and she's with poor Amelia, but if we don't do this I'll forget. Send her a message and ask her to close the shop for a few days. She knows where the family emergency sign is. I don't expect her to be able to work as long as Amelia's unwell and it'll be too much for just you to manage for a holiday weekend."

Tara quickly tapped her screen as Gran began flipping through the photos. "They didn't come out very clear," Gran commented as she flipped through. "There's something glowing in the center, but it's hazy."

"Video's the same," Tara said as she watched on her phone. "Wait." She stared at the screen eyes wide. "Watch this video."

She held her phone out for Gran to see. The video showed Marissa's perspective, and she described what she was seeing. "There's a large stone in a center of a ring of candles," Marissa said on the video. "Look what's all around." Rustling and the view blurred as she knelt down. She held a small object in her hand. They could make out a silver chain and a green gemstone.

"Is that jewelry?" Gran asked.

"Tons of jewelry," said Marissa on the video. She panned the camera to show necklaces, bracelets, and rings, all laid out on the ground. "That stone looks oddly familiar, though." They heard a scream. The phone fell. They heard and caught glimpses of a struggle and then the video ended.

"I told her not to go there!" Gran cried. "I knew she'd be caught."

"Maybe that's the trigger," Tara said as the idea dawned. She tapped the screen and zoomed in on a piece with a large green stone. "The jewelry! It looks like the stuff Mr. Moon was giving away. I was wearing that necklace I won the first time me and Henry went out. Amelia must have had something on, too."

"You think those are from Mr. Moon's shop?" Gran asked.

"Where else?" Tara replied. "Nobody else in town sells things like that."

"Perhaps," said Gran. "I believe Rose said she won a bracelet."

"I'm going to go see Mr. Moon in the morning," said Tara. She grabbed her bag and started gathering her belongings.

"What?" Gran exclaimed.

"Those pieces look like they came from his shop," Tara explained. "Why would his jewelry be in an enchanted circle? And how come the people wearing those pieces are getting sick?"

"What if he doesn't have the answers?" Gran demanded. "Or what if he does and you end up like Marissa?"

"I'm not even going to bring up magic. I just want to ask him questions about where he got them and maybe that will lead to answers." Tara asked, and ran out without another word.

∼

As Tara reached the waiting room, she heard shouting coming from the halls. Mr. Moon burst in, tears streaming down his panicked face. "Please, someone help me!" He raced to the registration desk, where Sally calmly met him.

"What's wrong, Mr. Moon?" she asked.

"It's my wife," he said. "She just... Oh God!"

Sally and Tara led the weeping man to a long bench. He continued to hold his wife as he struggled to stop the sobs. Tara filled a foam cup with water from the fountain and handed it to him. He sipped, sputtered, and then managed a few deep breaths.

"Alright, Ethan," Sally said. "Tell me what happened."

"We have a little rooftop space on our apartment above the shop," he explained. "It's not much, but we have some things up there so we can sit and relax. Great view of the town. Anyway, we were watching the fireworks. Ruby had just gotten over being sick and wasn't ready to be around people yet, but she loves the 4th of July, so we went to the roof. All of a sudden, she complained of a headache. We went back to our apartment and she just... dropped."

Tara glanced at the unconscious woman and noticed she was wearing one of the garnet necklaces. The stone still held a very slight glow. She wasn't sure if anyone else saw it.

A light bulb went off in Tara's mind. Leaving Mr. Moon in the care of Sally, she raced to Marissa's room. She saw it immediately. A faint glow near her head. Marissa was wearing her earrings that she won at the opening of the jewelry store. Tara removed them as carefully, but quickly as she could. She felt that force again and the weakness that followed. Once they were off, she set them on the floor, grabbed a chair, and slammed it down on the earrings in two successive clangs. Sparks flew and the subtle glow suddenly became blinding. Tara shielded her eyes. When the glow faded, the gems were cracked in half and the sparkle was gone. They looked like ordinary green rocks.

Marissa shot up, gasping for breath. "What the hell!"

Tara, eyes stinging with tears, pulled her friend into a tight hug. "You're alright! Oh my God, you're alright!"

"Yeah, but I won't be for long if you crush the air from my lungs," Marissa gasped.

Tara stepped back. "Sorry." She told her what Mr. Moon said and what she saw in the waiting room.

"We need to get back to your house," Marissa said. "You have that necklace?"

"Yeah, it's in my jewelry box."

"Good, we can use it. I'm going to have to pull some tricks from my hat to get out of here. And we'll need to recruit some help."

CHAPTER 15

Tara pulled her car around to a side entrance of the hospital and Marissa got in. She had found a green hoodie, put it on, hood up to hide her face and slipped out. Only thankful she was not hooked up to any IVs. They took off to Kavanagh House. Afraid touching it would trigger the effects of the necklace, Tara grabbed the jewelry box from her room and they drove to the Apothecary.

"It's like 2 in the morning - she won't be there." Tara said.

"She has an apartment above the shop. We are going to need all the help we can get to destroy this thing," Marissa explained. "Shylah knows her stuff and is extremely powerful. With Gran incapacitated, we need her. Trust me on this." She scooped up a handful of small pebbles and tossed them one by one toward the windows.

After a few taps, a light flashed on revealing a very sleepy Shylah who stuck her head out the window. "Wha'sa matter?" she called out, groggily. "Where's the fire?"

"Shy! Down here!" Marissa called out, waving her hand. "Let us in. Big bad mojo going down."

Shylah seemed to jolt awake when she realized who was calling to her. "I'll make tea." She quickly shut the window. Locks on the door clicked and Marissa all but pushed Tara inside.

They headed up the stairs to a plain wooden door. Shylah opened it immediately and invited them inside. Tara looked around as Shylah made the tea while Marissa filled her in on everything. It was a decent size place for a single person. A kitchen, bathroom, bedroom, nice living area divided into a living room, dining room, and office space.

Every room was painted in vibrant colors. The kitchen was yellow with sunflowers painted along the top. Herbs dried by the window adding the scent of cloves, basil, and rosemary to the room. There were also hand painted plates displayed on a shelf that just added to the warmth of the space. The living room was an almost pumpkin orange. Curtains embroidered with flowers and jungle scenes hung from the windows. Tara figured Shylah brought them and the plates with her from India.

The best part was the living area, almost entirely covered in bookshelves except for where the windows were. In the dining room, there were mostly cookbooks. The office had a lot of business books sprinkled amongst file folders and tattered binders. Tara was pretty sure Shylah's book collection would rival Gran's.

"Are you a bibliophile, too, Tara?" Shylah asked as she came in with a tray of tea, ornately designed little teacups, and cookies.

"Yes, I'm a huge book lover," said Tara. "I love Gran's library. I have what I thought was a pretty hefty collection of my own." She gestured around her.

Shylah laughed. "A lot of these are from family." She pointed to the cookbooks. "One of my aunts collected old recipes from all the great-aunts and grandmas that had been passed down since forever, had them printed and bound and made everyone copies. Ended up being several volumes. I think she has a couple more in the works. They have stories in them along with recipes. So, it's like a little time capsule."

"We can drool over books later," said Marissa. "We need to get down to business."

Tara sipped her tea, stifled a wince at the initial surprise of the strong flavor, and opened her jewelry box to show Shylah the necklace. "Don't touch it," she warned. "If it's touching you, that's how it works on you. It will suck on your energy and drain you."

"We have learned it has to be triggered somehow," said Marissa. She pulled the shattered remains of the earrings. "I was wearing these all day and nothing... until I decided to get reckless."

Shylah looked closely at the necklace. "Are they an Emerald?"

"Green garnet," said Tara.

"Didn't you come to Mr. Moon's opening?" Marissa asked.

"I wanted to," Shylah said, examining the box. "I couldn't close up that day. Had a bunch of orders I needed to fill. I came when people started getting sick and they needed my help." She continued to look at the jewelry box. She picked it up and looked from all angles, careful not to touch the necklace. "Interesting..." She stood and began looking through her books. She pulled out two from the shelf. One on color magic and one about gemstones. She flipped through until she found the page on Garnets. *Garnet is the stone of regeneration. It cleanses the soul. It was said to help warn of danger and was carried long ago as a protective talisman.*

"But, it's mentioned in this book," she held up the color magic one, "that the opposites on a color wheel can determine an opposing response in some items if the right spell is used." She flipped a few pages and showed them a page of a color wheel. "So, a garnet is traditionally red, right?" Tara and Marissa nodded. "Look at what the opposite of red is on the wheel."

"Green," Marissa and Tara said nearly in unison.

Shylah nodded. "You both get a cookie. So, by this logic, the garnet would go from re-energizing and protection to draining and open to harm if it were green."

"So, how do we undo it?" Tara asked.

"Destroy the main stone," said Marissa. "That's the heart - the main link to all of this. That has to be why the other pieces were around it. It was sort of channeling the energy, charging the cut pieces."

"How do we do that.. destroy the stone?" Tara asked.

"Well, as long as we have at least one link," Shylah explained, "we may be able to channel the spell through it. It'll take a great amount of power and consideration of what the ritual looks like. One wrong move and it'll blow up in our faces."

"So, we better get working on it," said Marissa. "This should be done as soon as possible otherwise whoever is doing this will increase the power of the attack or scamper off."

"Did you happen to catch a look at them?" Tara asked.

"No," said Marissa. She clenched her fist. "Son of a bitch came at me from behind. I could tell it was a man… I smelled his cologne and heard his panting breaths. And, he's strong."

"I'll grab some of my books and get the ingredients," said Shylah. She went to a closet and grabbed a large navy blue backpack. "We should do it outside at Kavanagh House. I have no yard and doing spells like this is best outdoors. And, it's too dangerous to go back to the site. I'm sure Mrs. Kavanagh won't mind us using some of her things to fill in the gaps."

Draining the last of their tea, Tara and Marissa helped Shylah gather what she wanted. When they were outside, Tara noticed Shylah examining the moon.

"Full moon would have been optimal, but we're a couple days late," she observed. "We'll have to work with it."

They piled into Tara's car and returned to Kavanagh House.

CHAPTER 16

WHEN THEY RETURNED TO KAVANAGH HOUSE, SHYLAH dove into the books while Tara helped Marissa set up a space. They found every candle and crystal that symbolized protection they could get their hands on in the house and arranged a large circle in the yard, alternating between candles and crystals. The crystals twinkled in the light of the moon overhead. Marissa lit some incense and walked around the space reciting a cleansing spell.

"Blessed Mother, hear our call.

Protect us.

Guide our hand in the work we are about to do.

Purify this sacred space and guide our hands

As we work in your name."

"Not taking any chances this time," she told Tara when she was done.

Tara nodded. "I don't blame you."

Shylah called them over to her makeshift altar at a picnic table. She handed Marissa a sheet of paper. "Read over this. See if you think it needs tweaking."

Marissa took a red pen, read over, made some notes, and Shylah wrote some more. Tara watched them work, trying not to look anxious or show how truly out of place she felt. They heard the early morning birdsong starting. "We're running out of time," Marissa said. She turned to Tara. "When Shylah's done, we're going to say the spell 3 times."

"Why three?" she asked. "We did that with the other one with Gran."

"Three is a powerful number in many practices and religions," Shylah said from where she worked. "You're Christian, right?" Tara nodded. "So, the Trinity. God is made of 3 people. Three days to the Resurrection. In Wicca, there's the triple goddess."

"Definitely something to read about more," said Tara. "You know, when our friends and family aren't in insane danger."

"Good idea," said Marissa. "I can loan you some books."

"Okay, we got it," said Shylah. She handed her friends a copy of what she had written. They quickly placed the necklace in the center of the circle and started the ritual. They started by casting a circle for added protection. Marissa led them in, picturing a brightly glowing light, and then feeling the energy rising up into a dome around them, like a protective shield. When that was done, Shylah recited a prayer on top of it in her native language to one of the deities she was devoted to.

They held hands and envisioned the area. Marissa explained the details to help them. The clearing, the trees, the giant green stone surrounded by black candles. It came to Tara's mind as clear as if she were there.

Once they were ready, they recited the spell three times.

"Burn fire, rise smoke,

The gods and spirits we call,

Let this evil sent be

returned from where it came.

Burn fire, rise smoke

Destroy the source of harm."

Nothing happened.

"Keep your eyes closed," Tara heard Shylah say. "Focus on the intention behind the words when you say them. Let's try reciting the spell again."

They repeated another round of three and the ground shook beneath them. The stone split with a mighty crack! Still glowing ominously. "Almost! One more round might do it!" she heard Marissa say.

When a dark shadow fell over them and a force of power hit them hard, Tara felt herself pulling away from the other two. She could sense Marissa desperately using all her strength to cling to Tara. She heard her name being called, almost a faint echoed screaming in her head, but she couldn't hold on to it enough to place the source of the noise and she slowly dropped away into nothingness.

～

When Tara opened her eyes, the sun was high in the sky. She shielded her eyes from the glare and looked around. Details came into focus. Trees, grass, but no garden. No house, no Shylah and Marissa. The place did seem familiar. She stood and turned around. This looked like the clearing from her dream with the blue bonfire.

"Hello, Tara," said a woman with a familiar sounding accent. Tara whirled around to see a middle-age woman in a simple white dress. Her bright green eyes sparkled, accenting her long, red hair that flowed freely in the wind. "My name is Lora," the woman continued when Tara just stared.

"Do I know you?" Tara asked, a familiar feeling washed over her.

"I'm your great-great grandmother."

"You–you're Granny Lora?" Tara gasped. She forced herself to look away for a second, so she didn't appear like she was staring. "Oh, God. Am I dead? Did I die? Is this, like, witch heaven or something?" She pinched her arm hard and then cried out. "Nope, not dead. But also not dreaming?"

"No child. You are not dead," said Lora, smiling kindly. "But, you are... well, currently unconscious."

Tara leaned against the nearest tree and heaved a huge sigh of relief. "So, why am I here?"

"You know you must stop this threat," said Lora. "Before more people are hurt. This is an attempt to strengthen an old evil force. If they are successful, your journey will be wrought with more challenges."

"More challenging than passing college?"

Lora ignored the comment. "Your journey as a witch and exploration of your abilities is only just beginning. If you choose to continue, you must accept there will be hardships and choices on that path."

"Ah, great. Cryptic. I should have known," Tara said out loud. "I'm not strong enough to do anything. I've only had a couple weeks to learn and I'm not ready to start defeating the big, bad, monumental uber evil," she said out loud.

"In a time of need, call on the strength of those who came before," said Lora. "They, especially of your blood, are always there when you call."

"What's that supposed to mean?" Tara asked. But everything around her started to blur and with a whooshing fade, pulling her into darkness. She called out for Lora to wait. She had more questions. But, once again, everything went black.

~

Light began piercing at her eyes. Tara sat up again, and she was back at home in the garden. As soon as she was upright, though, she was knocked back as Marissa flew at her and hugged her tight. "Oh my God! Oh my God!" she cried.

Tara struggled and strained. "Hey, I love you, too, but this really hurts."

Marissa pulled back and tears welled up in Tara's eyes when she saw the relief and joy on her friend's face. She pulled her back into a hug. "Where's Shylah?" Tara asked when they stopped. Marissa gestured as the sound of someone being sick echoed from the hedges beyond. "Ah, got it."

"She's been doing that for a few minutes now," Marissa said. "What happened? I thought we had it."

"I guess… we got caught again," Tara said. "And they were obviously pissed." She turned as Shylah returned to the patio.

Marissa handed her a bottle of water. Shylah held the bottle up to toast them and chugged half the contents. "Hope your Gran doesn't mind some… unconventional fertilizer in the garden," she said with a smirk. "That was… oof."

"To say the least," said Tara. "What happened when everything unraveled?"

"I felt like I was dropped onto my ass," said Marissa. "Had the wind knocked out of me. Shy, obviously, had to go lose her dinner. And you were just there… on the ground."

"Apparently, that was the only way I could get a message from my great-great-granny," Tara said. She explained her vision and Lora's message. "Of course, I have no idea what she actually meant. She had to be cryptic."

"The Litany of Witches," said Shylah. She bounced up and down, waving her arms. "Lightbulb moment! Why didn't I think of that?"

"Is that like the Litany of the Saints?" Tara asked. Shylah sent her a questioning look. "I was raised Catholic. It's a chanted prayer calling on all the saints to intercede."

"I suppose it's a similar idea," said Shylah. "This is more of a call for direct strength. It's not a common practice, but I've heard it can be very effective, especially when ancestors are included."

Marissa jumped to her feet. "Let's do it, then! Is it in one of the books?"

Shylah shook her head. "I've never seen it written down so we might have to write it out. I guess I have an idea how it goes, though."

As they worked, the sky began changing from dark blue to the purples and pinks of morning while sunrise grew closer. They agreed they probably had enough strength left for one more attempt, so they better make sure it's an effective one.

Once everything was arranged again, Shylah handed them each a sheet of paper with the new spell written on it. "I'll lead and then we'll do what we did before."

They each took their place within the circle. Shylah took a deep breath and began to speak.

"We call upon the power of the past,

We call upon those who have come before,

Blessed ancestors, we ask for your strength.

Lend us your power!"

Marissa continued. "I call upon Emily, Marie, Juliette."

"Sisters, hear our call."

Tara took up the chant. "I call upon Lora, Brigid, Madeline."

"Sisters, hear our call."

Finally, Shylah finished the round. "I call upon Sita, Anya, Rin."

"Sisters, hear our call."

They continued around two more times, calling out the names of their ancestors. As they spoke, Tara had the warming sensation of hands being laid on her back and shoulders, and indistinct whispers slowly surrounded them. She forced herself to keep her eyes closed to not break her concentration.

As light filled the yard, they recited the other spell three times over, pouring everything they had left into the words and intent of it. The surrounding voices joined in, a haunting chorus that sent goosebumps up Tara's arms and legs, but she forced herself to focus.

The image of the stone flashed in their minds. It glowed, an eerie, mysterious haunting green and then CRACK! The light spilled out as the stone blasted into a thousand pieces. A roar of rage drowned out the whispers. The ground vibrated, as if that voice was with them. The light went dim, and they all collapsed.

Tara managed to open her eyes for a moment. Lora stood before her, surrounded by other ghostly shadowed figures. She smiled. "*Well done, child.*"

Tara smiled back and letting the darkness creep back in from the exhaustion... then she passed out.

CHAPTER 17

TARA BLINKED AND SHE HAD TO ROLL OVER ONTO HER stomach. The sun shone brightly into her face. She sat up and took a moment to clear her head, taking in a deep breath of the fresh air... running her hand against her head which was now pounding. She saw Shylah and Marissa near her, also sitting up.

"How long were we out?" Marissa asked, swaying as she spoke.

"Judging by the sun, and how burned we all are, a few hours," said Shylah.

Tara looked down at her arms, wincing at how painfully red they were. She groaned as she got to her feet. She walked over to the picnic table and grabbed her phone. Marissa and Shylah went inside and she followed as she scrolled through the missed calls and messages.

"Oh damn," she said.

"What?" Marissa asked.

"I got fifteen missed messages from my mom," said Tara. "Our spell apparently caused a bit of a light show and Conspiracy Dude caught it on social media both here and in the woods. It made the news. He's got a huge post about alien communication."

"Oh wow," said Shylah. "He's slipping. That's the best he can come up with?" She handed Tara a jar of cream. "For the sunburn."

Tara finished looking through her phone. "I have fifteen messages and three calls just from my mother. Gran tried to call me twice and Henry tried to call." Tara said, letting a smile cross her face at the mention of Henry.

"At least just call Gran," Marissa suggested. "Everyone else we can sort out later."

"Better make sure you're not tagged in any of Allan's posts," said Shylah. "Or that he doesn't have a clear image of her house."

"Please, I don't think he would do that," said Marissa. "Give someone else any attention? No way."

Tara read one of the posts as she started to apply the cooling burn cream. "No, he didn't. He writes about the residents of Old Town 'sleeping peacefully unaware of the sinister plot by our potential extraterrestrial overlords.' Why do people believe him?" She scoffed.

"Ask your mom," Marissa muttered. "Make your call to your Gran. I'll put some of this stuff on your arms and neck."

"Thank you," Tara said as she tapped her screen.

"Put it on speaker!" Shylah said as she worked on some tea brewing at the stove.

The phone rang twice. "Tara?"

"Hi, Gran. How are you feeling?"

"You did it!" Gran cried. "You actually did it! Why do you sound weird? Are you okay?"

"You're on speaker," Tara explained. "I'm here with Marissa and Shylah. We all worked together."

"Hi, Ms. Kavanagh!" Shylah called loudly from the stove.

"Marissa's with you?" Gran asked. "You better have a good explanation. The doctors realized she slipped out and sent the police after her!"

Marissa crossed her arms and tapped her foot, looking indignant. "That's a bit overkill, don't you think?"

"Never mind that for now," said Gran. "What did you do? Everyone is waking up. I felt the effects spread through the hospital." They all started clamoring at once. "One at a time!" Gran said. "I'm in recovery from a head injury. I can only handle so much." She paused. "Dear God, I better not start acting like an old lady now."

"Says the lady in her 80s?" Tara said to her friends.

"I heard that!" Gran shouted.

They laughed and Shylah took the lead in explaining the ritual they came up with the night before. "It was brilliant," Marissa chimed in. "We did the spell twice and then got pushed back. You know like how it happened in the basement."

"And then I had a vision of Granny Lora!" Tara exclaimed.

"What?" Gran cried.

"I'll tell you more about it when I come see you, but she was beautiful," Tara continued. "And, I thought she was being all cryptic when she told me blood would always be there to help but then Shylah got the idea to do... what was that called?"

"The Litany of Witches," said Shylah.

"Yes," said Tara. "And it was amazing!"

"We actually heard our ancestors joining in!" Marissa added. "It was a rush!"

"That's incredible," said Gran. "I'm proud of all three of you."

"How are you doing? Tara asked. "When are you getting discharged?"

"The doctors said I can come home tomorrow," Gran said.

"I thought you said it was just overnight," said Tara.

"Yes, but apparently I busted my knee a bit more than we had thought so they want to make sure I can walk around normally and function without being on hyper strong pain meds."

"You refused to go to a nursing home, didn't you?" asked Marissa.

"I certainly did," said Gran. "I agreed to therapy. But, I am going home. Just sad I'll need to use a wretched old lady cane for a few weeks. I'll really look my age and then how will I snag a young rich man?"

"Just get some rest, and we can decorate your cane up a bit – give it some color to match your personality." said Tara. "I have to call home in a bit. What's the story?"

"Tell your father I'm fine and coming home," said Gran. "I don't want him worrying or spreading the word to the rest of the kids. I'm just bruised and sprained. Nothing that requires surgery or anything. It just hurts like hell."

"Alright," said Tara. "We'll come by to see you later."

"Yeah, I should go back and show them I'm fine," said Marissa. "I'm also going to give them a piece of my mind about sending the police. What even is that about?"

Tara ended the call and tapped her screen to call Henry next. This conversation was brief. He had returned to the hospital after his mom was calmed down enough to sleep, but Tara had already left.

"I needed to sleep and get that paperwork done." was all she said.

He did have questions about Marissa missing that Tara artfully evaded. "Be glad Aunt Sally wasn't her nurse," he said. "She would have been caught for sure."

Finally, the time came for Tara to call her mother. She listened to the crazy rant about the video from the Conspiracy Guy. "Mom, how many times do I have to tell you? He uses special effects to sensationalize his videos and get clicks."

"Why would he be recording in that area of the neighborhood?" Mom demanded.

"I don't know," said Tara. "Marissa says he's a creeper. Maybe he was looking for something or was bored?"

"Tara, I've tried to be the supportive mom, but I would feel better if you would come home. That place is horrible. I can help you find another school or you can go where your dad teaches for a while."

"I can't do that," Tara argued. "I can't just bail on Gran. And I'm making friends here."

When she still wouldn't let up, Tara said, "Mom, I have to go to work. I'll check in tomorrow!"

They drove back through town. First stopping to drop Shylah off so she could nurse her own sunburns and go to sleep. Then they went back to the hospital. Marissa walked in separately, so Tara didn't get in trouble helping her escape. Tara went to Gran's room and was greeted with a big smile.

"I'm so proud of you, Love," she said.

"Thanks, Gran. Once I've slept, I'll try to write everything down. I don't want to forget this." She hesitated for a minute. "There's one thing I forgot to tell you over the phone." She told Gran once more about the vision of her Granny Lora. "She looked younger," Tara said. "I guess she can appear however she wants. But she was beautiful, just like the pictures you showed me. And, I could feel that she was holding my hand as we finished off the spell."

As she told the story and described everything, a tear rolled down Gran's cheek. "Are you okay?"

"I'm so happy she came to help," said Gran. "I always believe she's looked out for me in her own way and now she's helping you. Even if you decide not to continue learning. I know I made a promise not to pester you about it until school started."

"Actually…" Tara began. "I think I want to. Last night was scary, but we helped a lot of people. I'll have to figure out how to tell Mom and dad but let's get through summer and my first semester to see how I can cross that bridge without it falling apart underneath my feet."

"Agreed," said Gran. A smile etched onto her face, highlighting the lines and beauty of her age.

He roared as he threw a chair across the room. Ruby lay in the hospital bed, lifeless, but monitors remained normal.

"I'll kill them!" he screamed. "I'll kill them all! Slowly! I'll let them linger for weeks… months! I'll…"

"You will LEAVE THEM BE." She demanded in her melodic voice.

He whirled around and froze as his heart went straight to his throat. Lilia stood in the mirror, beaming at him. She winked and reached out a hand. The surface of the mirror rippled as if she had touched a pool of water. He reached out a shaking hand, their fingers brushed then clasped.

She took a deep breath and stepped through, into his embrace. She wrapped her arms around him. He clutched her tight, taking in her scent, the texture of her hair. She was solid, flesh and blood once more. He moved his hands up and down, memorizing every curve. Their lips met. She grabbed a fistful of his hair. He bit her ear. She pinned him to the wall and nearly reached for his belt, but paused. She smiled at his bewildered look and stepped back.

"Not yet," she said.

"What?"

She nodded toward the dead woman in the room with them. "I cán deal with this." She stood over the bed, stretched her arms out and chanted. Slowly, the body faded away to nothing. He grinned when she opened her eyes. She thought for a moment. "Hmm, something still isn't right. People will notice." she said. She snapped her fingers and her features twisted and morphed until she looked exactly like Ruby Moon. Darien smiled. "If you can pretend to be Ethan, I can be Ruby. Then nobody will ever know," she said. She stood on her toes and gave him a peck on the cheek.

"I'll know," he said. "And that's all that matters."